THUNDER HEART

Book Two in the Mist Valley Series

MS. B. LAMPING

DEDICATION

This book is dedicated to all my co-workers in the medical community who prove daily that the art of healing is truly a gift of love, and my special author friend Mel Thorn, without whose expert advice and editing skills, this book would have never happened. Thanks also to my Granddaughters, Jessie and Michelle, for their enthusiastic praise and encouragement.
Special thanks to all those who contributed to my books cover. It was painstakingly put together with bits and pieces to create my idea for it.
Thanks with all my heart and undying love to all of you.

DISCLAIMER

This book is purely a work of fiction and any resemblance to peoples, real or imagined, past or present is completely by accident. This book, though set in an historical context, does not represent historical accuracy, as it is a work of the writer's imagination, and while the religious beliefs of the Cheyenne people have been well-researched, the writer has used the rights of the individual tribes to add or subtract from the way some of the religious beliefs were practiced to create the ceremonies in this book.

AUTHOR'S NOTE

This work was written to provide the reader a glimpse of native beliefs and family life, as well as to give them a peek at a world that has for so long lived in my heart.

Mist Valley was a visionary green valley my father was allowed to see before he died, and it's in that place that I believe his spirit dwells today. High on the mountain side in a cabin overlooking a lake in a valley of indescribable green, where men and animals live in peace and no one wants for anything.

Momma calls it Indian Heaven.

I call it HOME.

RECAP OF BOOK ONE: MIST WOMAN

SPRING 1886 IN THE CANADIAN ROCKIES

Mist Valley is a beautiful place originally owned by a white trapper and his Cheyenne wife, however it now belongs to their daughter Helee and a small tribe of Cheyenne who fled just across the Canadian border from the U.S. to escape being captured and possibly killed by the U.S. Army.

The Cheyenne and Sioux had fought long and hard to maintain their freedom, but in the end, they were defeated. Only a desperate few found their way to freedom to settle in Mist Valley, but even there, their way of life was forced to change.

The Cheyenne people had originally started out living in the Great Lakes area, but the white settlers flocked to their lands by the droves and pushed them further and further west. Once on the Great Plains, they quickly learned to capture and train horses, and they soon became some of the greatest horsemen of the Plains tribes. But within one hundred years, their lives were changed yet again, and the great Indian wars began. There were war atrocities committed on each side, but in the end, the U.S. Army turned its big guns upon sleeping villages, killing everything that moved before torching the dwellings, leaving the survivors without food or shelter. Many such massacres happened in the dead of winter.

Quiet Hawk, Helee's husband, was the son of a village Shaman, who having had a prophetic dream about one such massacre, fled north with his family and friends to a distant valley in the southern

Canadian Rockies where they were safe for a time. But after Helee and Quiet Hawk were married, the people were forced to leave Dream Valley to escape a devastating forest fire.

Traveling eastward to the other side of the mountain, the tribe settled on Helee's land and called their new home Mist Valley. They lived in teepees on the valley floor in the summer, and in six-sided cabins within the tree line of the mountain in the winter.

Their tribe didn't want to live like the white man, but Helee, their tribe's healer, and her husband, the tribe's Singer and Shaman, along with an ex-priest named Black Crow, taught the people new ways to survive in their mountain home. With buffalo now no longer a traditional staple; they now hunted elk, deer, wolf and bear, along with many smaller animals and birds. With hides at a premium, the people learned to depend on trade blankets and cloth, as well as other supplies brought to them by the Mounties and other traders and trappers that passed through their valley.

With less area for the women to forage, farming was again introduced into their lives, growing the same crops their great-great-grandparents had grown: corn, squash, and beans. Herbs, also scarce or different in the mountains and needed for medicines, were dug up and carefully planted in communal plots and tended to by all.

The tribal structure also changed. While there were still Chiefs, one main and many subs, there were now two councils; one for the women and another for the men.

The women dealt with issues related to their gender as well as about their crops and when to forage for nuts and berries and such. The men discussed issues pertaining to hunting, the defense of the tribe and what to do about any criminal activities within the tribe. The consumption of alcohol was frowned upon and the use of guns was rare. The men and boys were in charge of the breeding and cared for the livestock as well as the dogs that again played a vital role in tribal life. As in the days of old, the dog became a beast of burden, but instead of pulling small travois, they were harnessed into teams and pulled sleds, allowing men to travel and hunt in the deepest of snows and return home within a single day. This improvement to their lives was passed to them by the Mounties who in turn got it from the Inuit peoples.

Their village looked more like a small town now than an Indian village. They had a church, which doubled as a schoolhouse, called St.

Michael's, a trading post, a livery where sick animals were treated and housed in the winter, a grist mill and saw mill that sat next to the river, and a woodworkers shop where furniture, canoes, sleds and anything else wooden was made.

The Cheyenne were a talented, hard-working, creative, and resourceful people, and while their lives were being forced to change, their traditional beliefs were held onto firmly. Honor, chastity, truth, courage, generosity, and spiritual faith, along with a loving nature, were the moral values prized most highly by the people. Education also was becoming highly prized, as well as learning the English language. It was a way to keep their people from being cheated, and a way of taking advantage of the white man's vast stores of knowledge, especially in commerce, as well as the legal and medical fields.

This is the story of Helee and Quiet Hawk's eldest son, who grew to become their tribe's greatest healer.

PROLOGUE

Lightening cracked and spread across the sky as the great storm raged around him. The wind sucked the breath from his lungs and the driving rain lashed his body with icy bone chilling cold and searing pain. Her scream pierced the air, but died in the wail of the wind.

In a panic, he dove into the great sea, but finding its power too great, he was swept deep beneath the waves. His lungs burned from lack of oxygen as he fought to reach the surface, and when he did, he sucked in air with great heaving gasps. The sky glowed with a streak of lightning, and he was allowed a brief glimpse of a ship. Its masts were broken and it was quickly being swamped by the raging sea. Fear and panic gripped his soul as he heard the woman scream again. Her pitiful cry for help was the last thing he heard before the raging sea again dragged him into its depths. He fought to reach the surface once more, but he was drowning in fear, a fear just as soul-chilling as the icy sea around him. He opened his eyes as the lightning cracked, and he saw her. She fought the water, her hair and white gown floating around her. She saw him too, and reached a hand out to him as she sunk below the waves.

Thunder Heart was consumed with the need to save her. He fought the sea until his heart thundered like a hammer in his chest. His lungs burned from lack of oxygen and the cold numbed his limbs until they felt like lead, but still he fought to get to her. She was right there, reaching out to him. He could almost touch her fingers now, but suddenly the lightning cracked again, and he jerked awake. Gasping for breath, drenched with sweat, and shaking with fear, he tried to make sense of his surroundings. Finally, he caught sight of the faint glowing embers of his fire. He was home.

Shivering from a cold made worse by a body drenched with sweat, he stirred his fire back to life and added more wood. The dream was starting to fade as his heartbeat slowed, but he couldn't get the sight of the woman out of his mind. The dream was too real. She was too real. Dreams like this one couldn't be ignored. He would seek council with his great uncle Quiet Waters, the tribe's eldest Shaman and dreamer. He would help him sort out the dream's meaning and tell him what he must do about it.

Dawn brought bright streams of sunlight streaking through his doorway and clean, fresh air to his lungs as he went outside to greet the day. He found his great uncle sitting outside his home, eating a bowl of thick corn stew.

"Uncle, I need to talk to you. You know I have been having strange dreams for years, but last night the dream was so disturbing I still shake inside. I, for the life of me, cannot understand it."

"Sit, Thunder, and tell me your dream. We will seek the answers together."

Thunder sat and the dream spilled from him in a rush as his heart pounded within him, renewed by the telling. When he was done, he turned hopeful eyes to his uncle and tried to slow his breathing again.

Quiet Waters, after a long moment of thought, said, "I think the answer lies within you and deals with your future. I think you must go to your sacred place and seek the spirits. You must fast and think about your life and the decisions you have made in it. Your future cannot happen until you understand your past."

"Thank you, Uncle. As I have not yet eaten, I will prepare today and leave right away after I tell my family good bye."

Quiet Waters smiled a knowing smile at Thunder as he departed. He knew what the dream meant, and he knew it was Thunder's destiny.

It took until the sun was high in the sky before Thunder settled himself on the high pinnacle that overlooked Mist Valley. He dumped the wood he brought and started his fire. He repaired the sacred circle of stones and as he gazed out over the valley he raised his arms and said his prayers, giving tobacco to the six cardinal directions and asking for the Great Spirits' blessing on his quest. Once done, he settled himself before the fire and started contemplating his life.

CHAPTER 1: SPARROW

It was the Moon of Cherry Blossoms, and the yearly sun dance was fully underway. Sparrow Little Thunder, who had just turned seventeen, stood tethered to the sun dance pole. He had been dancing for three days without food and water, praying for a vision from the Great Spirit that would guide him for the rest of his life. He was always a boy set apart, teased and tormented by his peers because of his love of books and emotionally insecure in the shadow of his honored parents. He fought hard for acceptance. This ritual of prayer and physical sacrifice was a deeply religious and personal struggle he felt powerfully compelled to do.

The sun dance was an ancient ritual where the participants, after purifying themselves in a sweat lodge, had bone awls pushed under their breast muscles, and those were attached to long leather thongs that were themselves attached to the sacred sun dance pole that stood some twenty or thirty feet in the air. Then the participant was to sing his prayers and dance around the sacred buffalo pole, as it was called, while staring up at the sun, and if the pain grew too great, he would blow hard on a small bone whistle that was held firmly between his teeth.

This sacrifice of blood and pain would go on for many hours, or even days, until the supplicant yanked hard enough to rip the awls through his skin, thus freeing himself from his bonds. This ritual symbolizing rebirth was done to seek the blessing of the Great Spirit for the whole tribe, and was not done lightly. It was believed that the supplicant's pain, bravery, and blood would bring *Ma'heo'o's* (The Creator's) favor for all the people and perhaps a personal vision as well. Even though this ritual took place every spring, it was not mandatory for anyone to participate, but rather a very personal endeavor endured for very personal and sacred reasons. Sparrow had many questions he hoped the Great Spirit would answer for him. One of which was why he had nightmares of a woman screaming for his help as a great storm raged around her.

At the end of the third day of dancing, as darkness rapidly approached, Sparrow was beginning to feel his life draining away. With his head thrown back, staring towards the heavens, he summoned all his remaining strength for one last courageous effort to obtain freedom. Blowing hard on his bone whistle, he twisted with almost superhuman strength until his body was jerked free from its bonds. He stood wobbling for a moment as blood streamed down his chest to spatter upon the dust at his feet. Then he sank to his knees with his head hanging down. His sweat-drenched hair dragged through the bloody mud as he gasped for breath. Before the darkness finally closed in upon him, he raised his eyes again to the sky. Summoning all his remaining strength he punched his fist towards the heavens, and cried out *"Va'out, Ma'heo'o*, it is done!" Then he collapsed face-first onto the bloody ground. His body twitched as his mind was finally engulfed in a powerful vision.

While he lay there, unaware of his family's ministrations, his spirit floated high above his body in a warm, peaceful sense of belonging. He could see all of his people spread out below him. Then like a great bird spreading wing, he ascended high into the sky where he was surrounded by clouds. He could hear a great thundering as though from a great storm, but the clouds were not dark. As the thundering became louder, so did the thundering beat of his heart. Just when the thundering became so intense that he felt his heart would explode, the clouds parted and he landed on a hilltop overlooking a herd of Buffalo. He stood there gazing at the herd until the wind changed suddenly, alerting the animals, and as they raised their heads to the sky, a sudden bolt of lighting struck the ground, sending the buffalo stampeding straight for him. Sparrow didn't move. He just stood there watching as the panicked animals being led by a great white bull rapidly approached him.

Sparrow, feeling surprisingly calm, stood his ground until the bull suddenly stopped close enough to his face that he could feel the bull's heated breath as it snorted through its dark nostrils. He and the buffalo stood face-to-face and eye-to-eye for what seemed like an eternity before the buffalo, in a deep rumbling voice, began to speak to him.

"Son of Quiet Hawk," he said. "You will no longer be called by your old name. You will be called Thunder Heart, because your heart beats as one with mine and your buffalo brothers. This is my promise to you, Thunder Heart of the Cheyenne: I will forever be your brother, and if you have any need, you may ask it of me freely. Once you are healed from the wounds of your dance, you will go to the valley where my earthly body resides. Once there, you must kill me and use my meat to feed your people. Then, have your mother tan my hide for you to use as your blanket, always."

"But great one," Thunder Heart replied. "Your earthly body is sacred to the people. How can I kill you? Once you are dead, you will be dead."

"Do not worry about me, son of Quiet Hawk. I have left my seed within the heard. Tell your people to watch for my return, and when they see me again, it will be the sign that a great blessing is coming to them."

"It will be as you say Great One" replied Sparrow.

The Great Buffalo bowed his head and Sparrow was enveloped in a downy-soft mist that parted only briefly, allowing him a glimpse of the most beautiful woman he had ever seen. As he beheld her reaching out to him, he heard the old buffalo's words spoken softly as if from a great distance:

"She awaits you, Thunder Heart, Great Healer of the Cheyenne."

Sparrow, now called Thunder Heart, rose again skyward out of the mist that had surrounded him. He flew higher and higher, until he soared up and over the mountains to glimpse the vast ocean to the west. There he flew with the mighty eagles and watched as they swooped low to catch great wiggling salmon in their talons. He had never felt such feelings of freedom and peace before, but he was becoming tired. He began to feel heavy, as if he carried a great weight on his back, yet he continued to fly. After what seemed like hours, he descended back to earth where his body was instantly engulfed in searing pain. It was a pain so horrific that he instantly and regretfully knew his vision was over.

He struggled wearily past the layers of hot, searing pain to open his eyes. He saw that his family had taken him back home and his mother had dressed his wounds. At first he started to panic because the pain in his chest was so intense, but then he relaxed when he heard his father singing prayers over him and filling the dwelling with the fragrance of sweet grass and sage. Thunder Heart breathed deeply and forced his eyes to focus on the soft green eyes of his mother, and smiled weakly.

"Have you had a vision, my son?" she asked

He nodded slightly, and Helee, knowing he could not speak of it yet, gave him plenty of water and willow bark tea to drink for the pain and bid him rest.

As was the custom among the Cheyenne, the sun dancers would remain in their teepees until they rested and healed. Then after seven days they would go before the medicine men in the Council House and recount their visions.

And so it was for Thunder Heart, but he held back the vision of the woman from the council. He believed they would not understand its meaning because he thought her a white woman. There in the Council of Elders, he officially took his new name. However, needing to tell someone the full vision he saw, he decided to tell his parents.

That evening, as his family sat around the central fire in their teepee eating their evening meal, he told them.

"I am sorry, my parents, but I didn't tell the council my whole vision. I left out a part about a woman that I saw, but I feared they would not understand."

Helee, as she handed him a bowl of stew, placed a comforting hand on his shoulder and smiled knowingly at his father. Quiet Hawk stated matter-of-factly, "Do not worry about this woman my son, or worry about when or even if she will appear in your life. You will understand the meaning of the whole vision when it is time for you to know. Now describe her to me, son."

Quiet Hawk drew another long drag from his cherished soap stone pipe before placing the sacred object on its stand by the fire, and gave his son his complete attention.

Thunder Heart closed his eyes, and unaware of the soft smile on his face, conjured the vision woman to his memory and described her in vivid detail.

"She stood by the great sea, *A'te* (father), while great waves rolled and crashed around her. She wore the dress of a white woman, and when she turned to look at me, the wind blew her hair over her face and I was unable to see it at first. But as I struggled to get closer to her, the wind suddenly changed directions and revealed to my eyes the most beautiful woman I have ever seen. She had long brown hair, eyes the color of the sky, and when she reached out to me, I thought my heart would stop from want of her."

Quiet Hawk, sitting beside his son, gently patted him, saying, "We must sleep now my son, and I must think on these things you have told me." Thunder Heart, sighing deeply, went to his bed. As he closed his eyes in sleep, his parents looked at each other and smiled knowingly.

They had been lead to each other by strong visions and dreams from the Creator and felt that this would someday happen to their son as well. They believed that this woman by the sea would play a major part in their son's future life because his vision of her was so strong, but they also worried that if this woman was truly white, the tribe would never allow Thunder to become chief as was his birth right.

CHAPTER 2: A YOUNG HEALER

Thunder heart, at age twenty, was a tall, incredibly handsome, viral young man with deep blue eyes, a heavy frame covered with corded muscles that was kept in shape by hours of physical work, and raven black hair that hung straight and thick to his waist.

He stood a head taller than his peers, and while he usually wore a full suit of buckskins, he would bring forth many a sigh from the women when he wore only his breach cloth. And though he could ride like the wind and fire arrows faster than most, he preferred to be a quiet, humble student devoting many hours to the practice of the medical arts.

From his mother, he had learned about healing herbs, how to prepare them and when and how to use them. From his uncle by marriage, Black Crow, who was an ex-priest, he learned to read and write in not only English, but many other languages as well.

Black Crow was an orphaned southern Cheyenne who had been raised and educated by Jesuit priests, and he had many books with him when he came to live in their village. Despite the tribe's remote location, their children were given a good education. Thunder Heart loved to learn, often running after the visiting Mounties, begging them to trade for new books. One of the Mounties, named Sergeant O'Malley, who came through twice a year, always brought special supplies to trade, which included books of all kinds. The most prized items, in Thunder Heart's opinion, were the medical books. While many of the books were ragged with torn covers, the elders lovingly restored them by placing them in new hand-tooled leather covers before adding them to the library of the church, which also acted as their school.

When Thunder Heart turned twenty that spring, Sergeant O'Malley brought him the most precious gift of his life. His parents held a special feast that night, and before the whole tribe, his special Uncle O'Malley presented him with a brand new doctor's bag containing all the instruments he would ever need to become a great healer and surgeon. He also produced a second polished cedar latched box that contained the newest in medicines, as well as ether, carbolic acid, cat gut and curved needles for suturing. Thunder Heart was speechless as he stood to accept the gift with trembling hands.

"How can I ever thank you, Uncle?" he stated. "This is such a wonderful gift."

"Nah, me boyo, ye don't need ta thank me. This gift has come from yer whole tribe. I was just the fetcher. Thunder, I am very proud of ye, and am honored from this day forward to be calling ye doctor, as do they." Sergeant O'Malley gestured with the sweep of his arm to all the people standing around them.

Thunder shook the man's hand firmly, and with a shaking voice told his fellows thank you and pledged with his whole heart to become the best doctor he could so he could repay his people for this wonderful gift. When he sat down again beside his mother to enjoy the feast, she patted his leg and smiled lovingly at him. She saw the single tear he couldn't hold back, sliding down his cheek as he held the bag lovingly in his arms.

"We are all proud of you, my son." She said.

Thunder Heart was so choked up he could only nod, but after a while he relaxed and enjoyed what was his graduation party, because to his people he was now one of their healers.

After that day, he poured himself into memorizing his books and was always available to aid anyone in need, as well as teaching any of the children who wanted to learn from him. He was gentle, kind, patient, and always respectful, but deep inside he was very insecure about his abilities, often seeking his mother's aid.

CHAPTER 3: DANCING MOON

One day, as he walked along the river practicing his Latin, he heard the laughter of young women. He quickly hid himself among the reeds, but against tribal rules, continued to watch as they approached. He knew he shouldn't be looking and was about to reveal himself, but when he saw the naked form of one particular maiden, he couldn't bring himself to look away. He had always had the maidens show interest in him, but none of them stirred his blood, and there was one girl in particular he avoided at all costs. He called her Little Gnat because she was such a pest to him, but today he could not look away.

Her name was Dancing Moon, a young woman whose life had been saved by his mother when she was a baby, and she was to Thunder Heart the epitome of female perfection. She stood in the river with water droplets trickling down her bronze, luscious body, to drip off her hardened nipples. As she bathed, running her long fingers through her waist length, straight black hair, Thunder's body became instantly hard with want. He turned his eyes away, embarrassed by his reaction to her. She had been a childhood playmate, the little pest that liked to throw rocks at him before running away to hide or climb a tree and laugh at him. He hated being laughed at. He was always different, set apart by his standing in the tribe and picked on by his piers who called him "white eyes" because he'd rather read books than to be with them.

As he stared at Dancing Moon's beauty now, he wondered just when she had grown up. Suddenly, as more women came to bathe, he began to panic. Fearing that he might be found out and shamed, he rustled the reeds and growled fiercely. He watched, chuckling to himself, as the girls grabbed their clothes and ran away screaming. When he arose from the reed bed he was smiling sheepishly, all too aware of the hardened appendage tenting his breach cloth. He had to do something, quick. He couldn't go home that way. He dropped his breach cloth and leggings and dove into the chilly water. It was then and there that he decided that since he wasn't a child any longer, that it was time he took a wife. As he floated naked in the river, he made plans to pursue Dancing Moon's affections in the time-honored traditions of his people.

First he carved himself a plains flute to practice on so he could play his love song for her— that is, if and when she showed an interest in him. Then he got up very early one morning and waited along the path that the women took to the river for water. When he saw her approaching he ducked behind a tree quickly and hid. Once she had passed by, he came out from hiding and sat upon a nearby log to wait. He would wait until she came back, then he would ask to carry her water for her. It was a good plan, he thought, but as he sat there working on his flute, he began to worry that she had seen and rejected him.

He was about to walk away, when she approached carrying four water skins. As she drew near, he stood placing his knife back in its sheath and the flute into a pouch at his waist. She must have had her thoughts elsewhere, because when he stepped out onto the trail, she became so startled she almost dropped her water bags. Fearing she might drop them, or worse yet, fall, Thunder reached out to steady her. The skin of her arm was warm and soft under his hand and she blushed warmly as her eyes shyly met his gaze. Maidens were not allowed to speak to or be alone with any man, not even their own brothers. Chastity was strictly enforced and when passion sparked between couples, they married. That is, if the girl's father agreed and had not already arranged a marriage for her.

"Oh, Dancing Moon, please forgive me," he said as he released his hold on her. "I see you carry four skins, and because I have bothered you, may I carry two of them for you? I am headed back to the village anyway."

She lowered her head but did glance up at him briefly. She smiled shyly and nodded her head. Not saying a word, she handed him two of her water skins and they walked back to the village in silence, each stealing glances at each other as they walked.

It was the custom of the people that after a maiden became of age, she was not to associate with or talk to a man alone. She had to follow the rules of the tribe or be publicly shamed as a loose woman. But as all young people do, they found ways to skirt the rules.

Once back in front of her parents' teepee, he handed her back her skins and she, with eyes downcast, told him softly, "Thank you." She ducked quickly into the teepee and hugged her mother saying, "Momma! Thunder Heart has finally noticed me. I have loved him all my life and finally he sees me as a woman. I'm so happy." She giggled.

"Stop thinking about boys," her mother chided. "You don't want them to think you are a loose woman and catch you alone somewhere."

"Oh, Mother, Thunder Heart is not like the other boys. He has a gentle spirit and shows respect for others."

"We'll see, my daughter, if he plans to court you, but for now get back to doing your chores."

"Yes, Momma," she replied as stars and feminine dreams danced in her mind.

Thunder Heart walked away from the teepee with his face hot and his heart racing. He was so smitten by Dancing Moon that from the first moment he had beheld her naked, he completely forgot all about the woman in his vision. He was young and she was beautiful and desire canceled out all else, even his studies, which greatly worried his parents.

Two days later, as he sat beside the river practicing on his flute, his uncle Beaver, who had once been called Little Beaver, approached him. Beaver was not his true uncle, but a southern Cheyenne who had been adopted by his father's parents after the Blue Coats had left him orphaned at the age of nine winters.

Thunder Heart greatly respected his uncle, not only because he had trained him in the ways of the warrior, for no one was better with horses or faster with a bow than he, but because he was the true son of a great war chief and wise beyond his thirty years.

"My nephew," he said as he sat down beside him. "I see you have made yourself a flute, and the song it plays is sweet. Could it be singing for Dancing Moon?"

Thunder Heart, blushing, turned toward his uncle and stated, "How did you know?"

Beaver chuckled, "We have all seen you looking at her, and my wife has told me that she looks upon you also, but why Dancing Moon? Is she not the one you called *Meskeso* (Little Gnat) when you were both small because she was such a pest?"

Thunder Heart smiled broadly and blushed. "Yes, she was, but now it is I who wish to pester her."

Beaver slapped him on the shoulder and leaning close said, "Now, listen, *ceye*. This is how you go about it." Then and there, he went about teaching him the ways of women, how to win them and how to love them.

The very next day, he brought her family a rabbit. The next, he brought two. On the third, he brought a young doe, and so it went until with each gift he left she was filled with giggles. Then, one night under the full moon, he played his flute for her and it left her breathless.

She quietly crawled over to her teepee flap and upon peeking out, gasped as her heart raced in her chest.

There he was silhouetted against the central fire's dwindling glow. He sat cross-legged in profile with his flute to his lips. He played for her there as the moon's silver glow caressed his face and the wind spun his white feather along with wisps of his long hair into the night.

She sat just inside her door and listened raptly, her heart totally won as her spirit moved with the sensual sounds he played. When he finally stopped playing, she bid him softly, "Thank you Thunder. It was truly beautiful. Good night."

The next morning outside the teepee, she found a basket filled with beads, porcupine quills, shells, elk teeth, bells and feathers. This, to an Indian maiden, was the equivalent to receiving very expensive jewelry.

She knew that he was going to propose, and soon he would be bringing her a pony, and if she accepted it, they would be wed at the next full moon.

Three days before the annual sun dance, he invited her to meet him in the horse pasture. It was magical. They walked among the tall green grass and laughed at the foals frolicking around their mothers.

Seeing a cluster of purple and white lupines, Thunder picked some and handed them to her, and as she took them he reached up and touched her cheek, softly running his fingers over its rapid flush. He gently ran his thumb over her bottom lip and after their eyes locked for a few minutes she dropped her eyes and bolted away, leaving him there, his body hard and aching amid a swirl of warmth and butterflies.

That evening, accompanied by Beaver and his younger brothers, Thunder Heart brought her father three of his best ponies, which he accepted, and the wedding was set for the next full moon after the sun dance.

CHAPTER 4: THE WEDDING

It was a beautiful night for a wedding. *Hanhepi-wi* (Moon Woman) hung full and high in the sky, bathing the people in her silver light as the young couple advanced slowly to stand before the elderly shaman, Quiet Waters. Thunder Heart's mouth went dry and his blood pooled hot within his groin as he beheld his bride. She was so beautiful in her white doeskin dress, bedecked in elk teeth, long fringe that swayed as she walked, and beads sewn into the star pattern that lay seductively across her bodice. White goose down feathers adorned her long black hair that hung loose about her shoulders, and her smile was radiant. The most beautiful thing about her was her sparkling love-filled eyes.

Thunder Heart stood tall and proud, wearing his white outfit consisting of leggings with long fringe decorated with tiny silver bells and a matching tunic that was adorned in porcupine quills set in the medicine wheel design. A small medicine wheel, along with a white eagle feather, was fastened into a single braid that hung from the left side of his long brown hair, and everyone could see the love within his heart as he beheld his bride.

He did indeed love Dancing Moon, but it didn't stop his insides from shaking or the self doubt that ran circles within his mind. Fear and doubt; Thunder was always plagued by them. He reached out and took Dancing Moon's hand and felt it tremble. She was as scared as he, and this somehow made him feel better. He relaxed then, and leaned toward her, whispering into her ear.

"Don't be frightened, *mitawin* (wife). A bride as beautiful as you should be happy. Relax. I will be a gentle husband."

She looked up into his eyes and smiled before stating, "I know, husband. You can be no other way."

They exchanged their vows and were blessed by sacred smoke and prayer. When it came time for exchange of gifts, Thunder heart reached behind him under his shirt, and without letting his eyes leave hers, took out the belt he had made for her from the hide of the sacred White Buffalo, and tied it around her waist.

Dancing Moon reached up then with trembling hands and placed the most beautiful necklace she had ever seen around his muscular neck. It was a medicine wheel adorned by sacred stones that hung in the middle of a soft leather thong, and at the bottom of that hung a buffalo-shaped medallion made from beaten gold.

As he felt her tiny hands start to leave his neck, a broad smile filled his face. He grabbed Dancing Moon up against him, and with one strong arm lifted her off the ground to swing her around and around. He then raised one arm into the air, and to the sound of her giggles and his peoples' trilling, he let out with a loud Cheyenne cry— *yee yee a ya ow o o*— to the heavens.

When he sat her down again, he took her radiant face between his large hands and kissed her deeply. He knew that open shows of deep affection was usually not shown in public, but the life of the people was changing, and since he could not hold in his love for her any longer and his heart was over flowing with joy, he felt compelled to change with it.

It was Beaver then who slapped him on the back and said, "*Ceye* (brother), you will have much time to kiss your woman. Let us now feast before we all faint from hunger."

Thunder Heart felt so alive with his woman at his side, and as they joined the circle around the central fire, he felt for the first time that he was finally one of the people and belonged in this world. It was a oneness that he had never felt before, but he also felt a bittersweet sadness because he knew their simple way of life would be all too soon gone forever.

Once everyone was seated before the central fire, the women began to serve the food and the dancing began. The Cheyenne had a dance for everything because their dances were prayers and the Cheyenne were very spiritual people. The first to come out to dance were the children eager to show the adults their practiced skills. Next to come out were the different male societies with hunting and warrior dances praying for good hunts and strength and courage while defending their people. Then came the Shaman's dance, and a hush fell over the entire gathering. Thunder Heart had seen his father dance many times, and it always left him breathless. Quiet Hawk had painted his body with his sacred prayer colors and wore only his breach clout as he whorled and leaped. He sang his prayers to *Ma'heo'o* with all of his heart, making his performance this night of all nights exceptionally compelling as he poured his heart and soul out to the Great Creator.

Thunder Heart became so caught up in his father's leaps and whorls that he arose to his feet in a panic when he saw Hawk, for the first time, jump right into the center of the fire. Thunder stood with his heart pounding in time with the mighty drum as he watched his father kick sparks high into the air as the flames surrounded him, and remained awe struck as his father leapt back out of the fire again to land on one knee right in front of him. Then Quiet Hawk stood to his full height once again, raising his arms to the sky. He threw his head back and let out a piercing call that brought Chat Ta, the beautiful red-tailed hawk that was his father's spirit animal and life long friend, to swoop down. The magnificent hawk landed with unmatched grace upon the ground before him, cocking its head from side to the side in anticipation of his master's command.

Quiet Hawk gently picked up the bird, running his hand over its feathers and looked deeply into his son's eyes before he spoke loud enough for all to hear.

"Thunder Heart, my son. Chat Ta has a gift for you."

Thunder Heart looked at the magnificent red-tailed hawk perched on his father's outstretched arm and watched as the bird plucked a feather from its breast and held it in its beak.

"Take the feather from him, *nae'ha'na* (my son), and place it into your medicine bag to keep it with you always. In this way you will know, that no matter where you are, you are always in his heart, as you are in mine."

With a trembling hand and the sound of his thundering heart pounding within his ears, Thunder Heart took the preferred gift from the great sacred bird and bowed his head graciously before saying, "Thank you mighty friend. I will forever treasure your gift."

With that, the bird bobbed its head several times before rising once more into the sky. After which, Hawk slapped Thunder on the shoulder and the two men sat down next to each other to watch the women dance.

Dressed in their finest, the elder women danced first around the fire in a clockwise motion, using a side-stepping manner that swayed their long fringes back and forth while several skilled women twirled hoops, spinning them into ever-increasingly difficult designs. Then came the young maidens wrapped in their brightly-colored trade blankets, side-stepping around the fire, facing the people. Each woman stamped once, in time with the drumbeat, before stepping to the side. With heads held high and stoic faces, they stole glances at their loved ones as they danced. After they had made several circuits around the fire, each one came to a stop before the man of her heart. There she would dance before him until he reached for her and then she would throw her blanket around him to claim his love.

Thunder Heart gazed up at his new wife as she danced before him and was filled with desire. Unable and unwilling to hold himself in check any longer, he stood, and she opened her blanket to accept him. As her blanket enfolded them he whisked her into his arms and carried her home as the sound of drums and joyful trilling of the people filled the night.

Their honeymoon tipi had been set up in a secluded lush glen up river from the main village to give the newlyweds time to be alone, and though it was dark, Thunder didn't miss a step as he traversed the forest path.

Once inside their tipi, he sat her down to stand before him. Tears filled his eyes as he beheld her beauty that was made even more so by the soft firelight. Finally he took a deep breath and pulled her into his powerful embrace.

They tenderly ran their hands over each other's bodies and were reluctant to separate, but having to ready their lodge for the night, they did so. Once done they soon found themselves in each other's arms again. Thunder ran his fingers through her long, silky hair before gliding them down her cheeks and onto her slender shoulders. Dancing Moon gasped and flushed deeply as he pulled the thongs of her dress loose, allowing it to fall in a soft puddle at her feet. He gazed upon her then with such intensity and passion that it made her tremble.

She knew he could not keep himself from her a moment longer. So, with trembling fingers, she helped him take off his shirt, thrilling at the warmth of his skin as she stepped close to him. He gently wrapped his strong arms around her, pressing her body to his, and sighed deeply as he felt her hardened nipples against his bare flesh. She could feel the swell of his desire against her belly as he caressed her, and she melted within his arms as he ran his hands down her back to cup her firm buttocks. Throwing her head back, she moaned in pleasure as he kissed the pulse at her throat. Then looking deeply into his eyes, she slid her arms around his neck and kissed him deeply. Dancing Moon was a quiet woman of deep passion and her kiss sent Thunder's heart flying as the flames of desire rose within him.

Thunder didn't know just when he had divested himself of the rest of his clothes, but the next thing he knew, they were laying on their firs glorying in the feel of each other's bodies. He reveled in the sounds of her gasps and purrs as he suckled first one breast and then the other. He slowly slid his hand to the juncture of her thighs, where upon finding the bud of her desire, gently caressed it, allowing the pleasure to fill his bride with uncontrollable need. After he had brought her to climax, and he felt her slick wetness upon his long fingers, he positioned himself between her legs. As she lie there, chest heaving, muscles quaking, he took hold of her bottom, drawing her closer to him, tilting her pelvis and positioning her legs to rest high around his waist. Then, holding his shaft, he slid its tip up and down between her slick folds, coating it with her moisture. She panted and writhed beneath him as he placed his shaft at her opening. Then, taking a firm hold of her hips, he penetrated her barrier with a single thrust. Her cry of pain was brief, yet it unnerved him, bringing him to pause. Brushing a single tear from her cheek, he kissed her with all the love and passion he possessed. More than ready for him to start their dance of love, she began to wiggle before he even started thrusting within her. This stoked the fires of his passion to soaring heights.

His Uncle Beaver had instructed him on the arts of love well, and all too soon, Dancing Moon lied quaking in ecstasy as he filled her with his seed.

Thunder Heart loved Dancing Moon with all his heart. She made him feel complete inside. She was the perfect submissive wife, having learned her role from childhood, but it was her respect of him as a man and healer that fired his love for her. They made love frequently, rejoicing in their passion for one another, often laughing and playing like children. They made love in the water after bathing, in the soft grass of the flower-filled meadow after dancing in the moonlight, and just when they thought their love couldn't grow any more, it did. Two months after their marriage, she was with child.

Thunder Heart was awe struck at the news, but upon seeing the sparkle in Dancing Moon's eyes, he dropped to his knees before her pulling her close laying his ear upon her abdomen, as if listening. Then without warning, he jumped to his feet and swept her up into his arms, twirling her around and around, laughing at her giggles.

"A son!" he shouted. "A son, *Ma'heo'o* be blessed, I have made a son!"

Dancing Moon laughingly replied, "You did not make a son my husband. We have made a baby. Maybe it will be a girl. Will you not also love her?"

Hugging her tightly, Thunder kissed her sweetly before saying with a chuckle, "A beautiful daughter. Yes, I will love her, especially if she is one who will make me a rich old man when the young men give me many gifts for her hand."

She just shook her head and smacked him upon the shoulder before saying, "Men! You are all alike. Why do you all want sons?"

"It is because we can teach them more things and we can share in their lives in a way that you, my wife, can share only with your daughter."

Dancing Moon nodded her understanding. "Now, my husband. Put me down so we can go tell your family and I can see what kind of teas your mother has. My stomach is upset." She giggled anew as he swept her up into his arms again.

"Husband, put me down. I am not broken." She held tight to his powerful chest.

"No, *mitawin*, I will not." He chuckled. "I want to enjoy this as long as I can, because soon you will become too fat for me to carry you."

She smacked him again and nipped his neck, but he only growled and held her tighter as he carried her all the way up the mountain path to his mother's cabin.

He set her down before the cabin door and knocked firmly.

When Helee opened her door he proudly stated, "*Nahko'* (mother), Dancing Moon has morning sickness and she needs some of your special ginger tea."

Helee looked at her shy daughter-in-law's rapidly spreading blush and hugged her lovingly before bringing her into the cabin. Thunder tried to enter, but Helee held him back with a hand to his chest and told him to go tell his father the news and that she wanted him to bring home two rabbits for their supper.

Thunder departed, hiking far into the trees before he found his father by the mountain stream, meditating. "*A'te* (father), I have wonderful news: Dancing Moon is with child."

Quiet Hawk looked up at his son and smiled broadly, silently bidding his son to sit and enjoy the sun's warmth while his carefully-placed rabbit snares did their jobs.

An hour later, the men returned to the cabin and the women prepared the celebration meal. The family spent a lot of time discussing what Thunder needed to do to prepare for the coming of his child while his siblings teased him about becoming an old man.

Later that night Thunder made soft, tender love to his wife and while she lie naked beside him basking in the afterglow, he placed a tender kiss upon her abdomen and spoke words of love to their child. Still convinced she was having a son, he told him to grow strong and healthy. The next day, he went hunting. His son would need warm clothes for the winter and a lot of food if he were to grow strong.

Thunder Heart was a good provider. He rarely missed a kill shot and attributed this skill to the fact that he couldn't stand to see anything suffer. He also, with the help of the other men in the tribe, built a sturdy, warm cabin and storehouse well up into the tree line of their valley, and soon his little family had everything they needed to survive the long, cold, snowy mountain winters.

The months sped by and Dancing Moon grew big with child. As the bitter winter descended, she spent a lot of time sitting by the fire, sewing. She felt the child's first strong kicks while Thunder was away helping a family whose child had come down with a congested chest. Smiling to herself, she placed her hand gently on the swell of her abdomen and started to sing an old lullaby: "Bye, baby bunting, your daddy's gone a hunting, to get a rabbit's skin, to wrap his baby in."

Helee and Thunder's sisters came by often and even stayed with her, so she was rarely, if ever, left alone. This gave Thunder peace of mind and allowed him to concentrate on his patients and their recovery.

CHAPTER 5: TESTED

One cold November day, Helee came pounding on her son's door, franticly yelling, "Thunder, Thunder, open the door! I need your help!"

Thunder Heart ran to the door, jerking it open. Fearing something had happened to a family member, he fearfully asked, "What is it Mother?"

Helee burst through the door and headed for his table, clearing it as she spoke. "It is Little Fawn. I need your help. She cannot deliver her child." Opening his door wider, he bade a frantic Young Elk, who was holding his unconscious wife in his arms, to quickly come inside. The Young man went to place his wife on the bed, but Helee directed him to place her on the table instead where the light was good.

Taking his mother gently by the shoulders, he firmly asked, "Mother, what is wrong with her?"

"She has been in labor for many hours and her strength has left her," she replied.

Thunder Heart took charge and instructed Young Elk to hold his wife's head while he examined her. Dancing Moon gave him his bag and poured some water into a large pot to boil.

"Young Elk," he said. "I need to see your wife's body and place my hands on her and even in her. I must find out why she can not deliver the child. Will you allow this?"

Young Elk swallowed back his fear and nodded his affirmative reply. Thunder Heart poured some hot water in a bowl and washed thoroughly, drying his hands on a clean towel. He felt her stomach, pressing firmly but gently before laying his ear upon it to listen for the baby's heartbeat. Then he slipped his long fingers inside her to feel the position of the babies head.

Once done he wiped his hand on the towel again and spoke to his mother. "Her child is too large and its head is caught. We must decide what to do and quickly or we will loose them both."

Suddenly Young Elk whipped out his knife, saying, "I know what to do. I will cut the child from her. I can live without a son. I cannot live without my wife."

Thunder Heart took the knife from the panicked husband and looking at his mother stated excitedly, "That's it. We will operate. I read about it in my books. I will cut her open and remove the child and then we will sew her up.

Young Elk, suddenly looking stricken, asked, "Will she live?"

"I do not know," Thunder replied, "But I do know that we will lose them both if we do not try."

Young Elk nodded his understanding and Helee ran out of the house, searching for a messenger. Upon seeing her youngest son, Little Mouse, age seven, she told him to run home and beat upon the great drum, thus calling his father and Quiet Waters to come sing and pray for the woman and her child.

Swatting him on the bottom, she bid the child, "Now hurry, my Mouse! I chose you for this job because it is so very important. Now go!"

Once back in the cabin, Helee found that Thunder had cleaned and arranged his instruments and had started some sage-burning in a bowl. While the sweet smoke filled the air, he cleaned the woman's abdomen with soap and water and the wiped over it with whiskey. Then he repeated this procedure on his hands. Taking some slow, deep breaths to calm himself, he centered his focus on the task at hand.

Knowing there was no room for error, his cuts had to be quick and his hand sure. He passed his knife through the fire four times and then made the first cut. Then, using his mother's cleaned hands to hold the skin back, he made the second cut with quick assurance. With that, the sack of waters ruptured and Thunder reached into the woman's womb, taking a firm hold of the infant's legs and pulled the large baby boy free of his mother.

He held him upside down for awhile until the fluids drained from the child's lungs. Then he swatted him on the bottom, making him cry to assure he could breathe. Laying him onto his mother's lap, he cut and tied the cord before handing him to Dancing Moon to bathe.

Turning back to the woman, he took out his sutures, and after soaking them with carbolic acid, he began stitching her back up. Once the uterus was closed, he pushed the afterbirth from her and then stitched up her belly, dressing her wound. He had read of shock in his textbooks, so he and Young Elk placed Little Deer on the firs before the fire. Then after raising her feet to rest upon a foot stool, he covered her with a trade blanket.

Dancing Moon was so engrossed in the baby that when Thunder came to examine him, she missed the sweet smile on her husband's face. Standing beside her, he noticed that the boy's head was mildly distorted, but his color was good and he had a loud, healthy cry, so he felt that the child would have no lasting effects from his abrupt delivery.

Normally, Indian children were trained from birth not to cry, but because of this little one's close call with death, he was indulged. Taking a tendon thread, he retired the child's cord and cut it shorter before he re-wrapped him and gave him to his father. Young Elk took his son with trembling hands as tears fell from his eyes. Shaking his head as he gazed at his son he said, "I can't believe I thought I could have killed him. Thank you, Thunder, and thank Ma'heo'o for this blessing."

Helee and the other women cleaned up the cabin while Thunder, using cool water, bathed Little Deer's face. When he saw her eyes flutter open briefly, his heart was flooded with relief. So far, she had survived, but he would continue to watch over her until he was sure moving her would not harm her.

That evening, as the men sat around the central fire of their woodland village, the ceremonial pipe was passed and prayers were once again sung for the mother and her child, and thanks were also sung for Thunder Heart. He had performed his first surgery and it was perfect.

After four days of bunking with his father, Thunder Heart returned home, and Little Deer and the baby, whom they named Cries Loud, was taken home to continue their recovery there.

CHAPTER 6: TRAGEDY STRIKES

It was on a bright, sunny day in the month of deep snow that Thunder's world was shattered.

Dancing Moon had been so cooped up and bored waiting for the long snowstorm to pass that when it did, she ventured outside. Crisp, fluffy, white snow covered everything, giving it all a magical feel. Bundled in a warm parka that hung below her knees and wearing knee-high moccasins lined with rabbit fur, she didn't feel cold at all, so she decided to walk to the river to fetch her water and check her animal traps. She walked along the river path, enjoying the day. The sun was so warm upon her face and the sound of the snow crunching under her feet made her heart soar. Suddenly a snowshoe hare darted out from under a bush right in front of her, causing her to stumble. Helplessly she slid down the river bank, frantic, attempting to stop her sliding, but to no avail. She slid helplessly into the semi-frozen, fast-moving river.

The freezing water instantly took her breath away and sapped her strength as it soaked her clothing, increasing their weight ten fold. As she frantically reached out toward anything in her path to save her, her mind raced in fear for her baby. She let out with a powerful scream just as she finally found a sturdy enough grip that allowed her, with all her remaining strength, to pull herself out of the river. She collapsed, now exhausted, and sank into darkness, but not before asking *Ma'heo'o* to send Thunder Heart to take her home.

Thunder Heart had had a good hunt that day. He had killed a good-sized buck and was headed home when he heard the piercing screech of his father's mighty hawk over head. Raising his eyes skyward, he was overcome with panic. The bird was headed in the direction of the village. Something was terribly wrong.

Dropping his deer, he ran for the village as fast as his legs would go. When he reached his cabin and rushed inside, he thought his heart would stop when he did not find his wife. Rushing outside, he asked everyone he saw if they had seen her. After what seemed like forever, one elderly woman said Dancing Moon had headed to the river for water, but that it had been early that morning. No one, not even his Mother, had seen her since. With his heart filled with panic, he raced to the river. He could see the tracks she had left, and when they ended at the river bank, his mind snapped and he began running along the water's edge, calling out her name over and over. After he had gone about a quarter of a mile, he saw what looked like a small bear laying on the river bank, but at closer inspection he found it to be Dancing Moon.

His eyes filled with tears when he brushed her wet hair from her face to reveal her ashen color and blue lips. At first he tried to carry her, wet parka and all, but the weight was too much, and he knew every minute counted. He stripped off her coat, opened his and while clutching her still form to his chest, he ran as fast as his legs would go and did not stop until he was inside his cabin.

Seeing her son racing through the village clutching his wife, Helee was galvanized into action. Grabbing her medical bag of supplies, she raced to her son's dwelling just in time to see him lay Dancing Moon's lifeless body upon his buffalo robe. He quickly stripped off her wet clothing and began to rub her arms and legs vigorously. He laid his head on her chest and listened for a heartbeat, but heard none. As Helee entered the warm cabin she saw her son holding his wife to his chest, pleading to the spirit of the white buffalo to save his wife and child. Tears streaking down his cheeks, he cried, "She is dead mother, Oh, *Ma'heo'o* I have lost them."

"Look, my son!" Helee shouted while pointing to Dancing Moon's abdomen. "All may not be lost. Your child is moving. If we hurry, we can cut him free and he may yet live."

Thunder Heart looked stunned, but when he saw the child's strong movement, he quickly grabbed up his knife. After passing it through the fire, he laid his wife back on the bedding, and began to cut his child free. The cuts were steady, and carefully made with love and reverence. Once she was opened, he reached his hand in and brought out his son. The child was blue, but he hung him upside down and firmly smacked his tiny back side. The child gasped and started to cry loudly. He cut the cord and handed his tiny son to Helee before returning to his wife.

Dancing Moon was indeed dead. Her face was blue, but she held a look of peace. As the tears streamed down his face he kissed her blue lips and whispered, "Thank you, my love, for my son. I will call him Winter Blue. Rest, *mitawin*. I will love you forever."

Consumed by his grief, tears streaming down his tortured face, he took out his knife and cut his wedding braid from his hair placing it reverently within her still fingers. Then with a primal scream, he slashed his chest allowing his blood to forever mingle with hers while he held her close.

When Thunder didn't come seeking his father the next morning, Helee sent Hawk to him. Hawk could hardly believe his eyes when he found his son. He sat covered in blood rocking his wife's body back in forth in his arms as if she were a child. Hawk was so overcome by the sight of his son's pain, he turned right around and gathered Beaver and Thunder's brothers to come and help him. Hawk was very glad for their help, as well, because even though he had spoken loving words of simple logic to his son, Thunder refused to let her go. In the end, it took all of them to pull him from her stiff form and drag him kicking and screaming into the light of day.

Finally, when Beaver had enough of his nephew's childish behavior, he slugged him up side the head. This, in combination with landing face-first in the freezing snow, brought him back to reality. Rolling to a sitting position, he sat there, defeated. His heart and soul shattered, he didn't even feel the cold, but he grudgingly agreed at last to be helped back to the family home where he sat by the fire, neither speaking or eating for three days

Dancing Moon was buried in the traditional way by being placed, while wearing her best clothing, on a scaffold that was hung high in the trees, and Winter Blue was given to a young mother who had just lost her newborn to be nursed.

Thunder Heart was changed by his grief, however. Swearing he would never love again, he threw himself into his studies, but the child of his heart was well taken care of and loved. Winter Blue eventually went to live with Thunder Heart's sister when his wet nurse became pregnant again. Thus Thunder was able to spend a lot more time with the boy, teaching him to be a good man of the tribe, which included going to school, but books did not interest Winter Blue. He was, however, a keen observer of nature and excelled with the horses, spending a lot of time with his great uncle Beaver.

CHAPTER 7: THE YOUNG HUNTER

Ten years had passed since Dancing Moon's death, but the pain of her loss was still an open wound within Thunder. Here on this ledge, overlooking the beloved valley of his birth, he didn't have to hide the tears that slide down his face. He loved this spot. He could see the entire valley from here. Its meandering river and herds of buffalo, horses, and deer never failed to bring him peace. He came here often to think, to speak with *Ma'heo'o* and pray for the people. On this day, he came to seek a vision. His heart was troubled and life weighed heavily upon him. His dreams were being tormented by spirits, and when he awakened, he could not remember anything beyond pain and fear. He had to have answers. Now he sat naked within a sacred circle of stones, wrapped only in his sacred white buffalo robe, chanting out his prayers and rethinking his life.

For three days he fasted, prayed, and did without sleep, but nothing happened. On the forth day of his vision quest, which was considered the holiest day of a fast, he suddenly heard an eagle's cry. He lifted his weary eyes upward and saw a huge bird descend and land right on the ground before him.

"What message have you brought me, brother Eagle?" Thunder softly asked.

The Eagle, with calm boldness, walked forward and bowed its head six times, before plucking out a tail feather and handed it to Thunder. Overcome with the sacred honor, Thunder, with hands shaking from weakness, took the preferred feather. Then, reaching into his war bag he produced a piece of smoked rabbit and offered it to the sacred bird in way of thanks. The bird accepting the gift, devoured it quickly, and then with the beat of its mighty wings, rose back into the sky to make one complete circle over his head before departing to the west.

Thunder Heart gazed at the eagle feather in his hand and smiled as memories of his past played across his mind. His childhood had been filled with joy and wonder as he played with his friends, and the many animals that frequented the homestead. He remembered the joy that the births of his three brothers and two sisters brought the family, but he also remembered how focused and singled-minded he had been. He wanted to be a hunter and a warrior once. So he practiced long hours with his bow until he could fire six arrows faster than most men could pull and fire a gun, and he was deadly accurate. He made his first big kill when he was ten summers.

He remembered how he was filled with pride as he walked, head held high, through the village with the hide and meat of the small deer he had killed, which he planned to share with the tribe, but to his Uncle Beaver, who had taught him to hunt so well, he gave the liver. He remembered how he had stood before his mother and father, chest puffed out and face stoic, even though he shook with fear inside as he sought their approval. Quiet Hawk nodded and placed an approving hand on him while his mother, with tears in her eyes, took the meat and hide and praised him for being a great hunter. She examined the hide and stated that she would make him a new tunic and that tonight he would stand before the Council fires and dance out his hunt.

He was so proud then to be called a hunter of the people.

He remembered how he pushed to grow up fast. Quiet Waters, his great uncle and the elder Shaman of their tribe, told his parents that he had an old soul and his growing up fast was a good thing for the people. Thunder pondered again the consequences of growing up faster than his peers; of how, out of his deep insecurity and desire to please his father, he had pushed himself to excel at everything accepted by their gender. He had few friends except for his family and their close friends, though he was respected by all. So it was that he came up to this high place often to find peace, to pray, and even cry out his loneliness.

He remembered how at the age of twelve, he was sent out to survive alone in the wilderness to find his way home, bringing the hide of at least one animal back with him. Allowed to take only his knife on this quest, he felt no fear as he and his father rode side-by-side on this journey. He remembered all the lessons his father had taught him and took to heart all his Uncle Beaver had taught him as well. How he had relished this time alone with his father listening to his advice. Survival was only a part of this rite of passage. He was to use all his skills as well as to listen and rely on the spirits if he were to return home safely.

They had ridden for three days ascending high into the mountains where he was left without food or water, wearing only his breach cloth and moccasins. The weather was pleasantly warm that first day as Thunder heart started the long walk home, but this was not a pleasure hike. He had to be aware of his surroundings. Every sound, every smell, the color of the sky, and the forest itself became of utmost importance to him. By midday he found a small stream which he decided to follow. Keeping the stream to his left, he continued onward, snacking on berries that he had found on his way. By evening, he had found a good place to camp in the shelter of some over-hanging rocks. Feeling protected by rock on all sides but one, he set about digging a fire pit and found enough wood nearby to last the entire night. Knowing that the mountain nights could become cold quickly, even with a fire, he collected an abundance of leaves as well to use as bedding and cover. So that first night he, though hungry, slept warm and comfortable.

By midday the next day, he knew his luck had run out. There were storm clouds in the northwest and the temperature was dropping fast. He veered away from the stream so as to shorten his journey, but he knew he couldn't outrun the storm. Breathing hard from climbing, he located a small cave, and had only just found his firewood when the storm hit. He remembered how he was so wet and cold that he thought his teeth were going to chatter out of his head. While he was in the process of starting his fire, he heard the snuffing of a bear. He froze then, and prayed that the bear would leave, but it did not. The bear, seeing him, became enraged and stood upon its hind legs, growling loudly. It just wanted to drive the smelly human from its shelter, but Thunder had no way out, and when he did try to get past the bear, it attacked him. He pulled his knife, and with all his strength, defended himself. He knew he had only one chance to strike at the bear, so he took his stand, and even though his heart hated the idea, he knew it was kill or be killed. Suddenly on his back with the Bear standing over him, its mouth a gaping black pit of teeth and drool, he grabbed a thick branch from his stack of firewood and jammed it into the bear's jaws with one hand as he stabbed the bear in the heart with the other. The bear struggled some after that, swiping its claws across its chest before it dropped like a stone upon Thunder's legs.

Still struggling for breath, Thunder pulled himself out from under the bear, and using the last of his energy, set about quickly to make a fire before going outside in the rain to clean his body and his wounds of dirt and blood. Once back inside the cave he collapsed beside his fire and thanked all the spirits for blessing him so greatly. After he rested for awhile and got warm, he gutted the bear and placed the liver on a spit over the fire. He tossed the remaining entrails outside, away from the cave so nothing of the bear would be wasted, thus ensuring that the spirit of the bear would be properly honored.

Smiling as he gazed out over the valley below, he remembered how well that meal had tasted back then and how, after he had eaten his fill, he had curled up next to the bear's thick fur and slept well. The next day, he recalled, had been cool, but the sun warmed him as he set about making a travois to carry his trophy home. After struggling with the animal he soon realized its weight was just too great for him to carry. So, he set about skinning it, carving off the meat and wrapping it back up into the hide, leaving its heavy, bony carcass for its animal brothers. He also saved the bear's teeth and claws. These he had placed in his medicine bag before heading again toward home.

Thunder Heart fingered the bear claw necklace at his throat as he remembered how his father, Quiet Hawk, had later stated that it was the hardest thing he had ever done to leave his son alone in the wilderness, and how he had sacrificed and prayed day and night until his son returned home. Quiet Hawk stated he had been filled with pride and relief that day when he heard the loud cry throughout the village as Thunder returned home, walking tall and dragging a travois piled high with the remains of a small black bear.

Never before, in the memory of the people, had there been such a young hunter. The council met that night, and when they called Thunder before them, he was so scared he trembled inside, but he kept his face stoic and didn't allow them to see his fear. He stood tall and proud before the council, but it was seeing the pride within his father's eyes that filled him with joy. And thinking back on it now, it was his father's approval that was really all he had ever really needed.

The old medicine man, Quiet Waters, had stood before the council fire, stooped, shouldered, leaning heavily on his walking staff, and spoke to him. "Sparrow, son of Quiet Hawk. You have proven yourself as a hunter and now as a man of the people. You must now pick a warrior society."

Thunder Heart dropped his head and thought of his teacher, Beaver, and stated, "I humbly asked to be among the Sacred Bowstrings."

The Sacred Bowstrings were the society of warriors that, in time of tribal trouble, stayed behind to protect the women and children. They would often sacrifice themselves by fighting to the death to buy time for them to escape. To be a Bowstring was the highest of honors. One that would silence his peers once and for all; that he was not a white man bookworm, but a real man of the people.

He remembered well the anticipation and fear of that day as he watched the Council of Elders, each nodding in turn, as their agreement and how he was filled with an overwhelming sense of pride when his father also nodded.

Quiet Waters stated loudly then, "*VA'OHT*, it is done."

So, from that moment on, he became the youngest member of the Sacred Bowstrings, a true hunter and protector of the people.

CHAPTER 8: THE VISION

Thunder, still reflecting on his life, remembered how at the age of thirteen summers, he set about readying himself for his first vision quest.

Unlike his rite of passage from boy to man that tested his survival skills, this was a religious quest. It was believed that a man was not truly complete until his mind, body and spirit beat as one within him.

He had spent a lot of time with the elder Shaman, Quiet Waters and his father, asking them many questions. They had explained every detail to him and sat with him in the sweat lodge as he purified his body and prepared his mind. He feasted the night before he left, and unlike his survival quest, this time he would take with him his bow and quiver of arrows, his grandfather's knife, and his unpainted war shield.

After a restless night filled with troubling dreams he finally got up before dawn and headed out at a brisk walk.

He climbed up to a high pinnacle, the very one on which he now sat. It was a perfect spot, a rocky ledge that over looked the valley below. He remembered how he had built his fire pit, and surrounded his sacred area with rocks that were cleansed by water and blessed by sacred smoke. With this done, the inner circle became his church, a holy place that would protect him, the seeker, from all evil harm. In this sacred area he would sit before his fire and offer tobacco to the six sacred directions; *Ma'heo'o*, the Great Spirit, to Mother Earth, and to the four Winds.

He sat there praying and fasting for more than four days, waiting for his vision. A vision in which he would see his spirit helper, who usually appeared in animal form, and it would show him things that would change his name, and set the direction he would forever follow in order to have a happy and complete life.

Thunder remembered how worried he was back then, because if he hadn't received a vision, he would have had to return home to try again next year. Thinking back on it now, he realized how much he was pushing himself, as most boys didn't do this quest until age fourteen, but he felt he had to find out why he was plagued by dreams and whether he should trust them as prophetic or not.

The first day had past as if it would never end, but he didn't falter in his prayers. He prayed for his people, his family, and all those of his nation who were held captive by the blue soldiers on miserable reservations without hope.

The second day he began to feel weak and very thirsty, but he didn't move from his area even when he heard a bear looking for berries close by. He just held very still as the bear came so close he could feel its breath, but it didn't cross the rock barrier. Instead, it nodded several times and left. That night the temperature dropped rapidly. Feeling the cold sapping his strength, he put more wood on his fire and stirred the sparks high into the air. He remembered that as his eyes followed the sparks skyward he had seen many falling stars shooting across the sky as the Aurora with its pinks, blues, and greens danced in the northern sky. He knew the spirits were close. He could feel them in his soul, see them in the sky, and hear their voices on the wind. He had floated with them that night, his spirit drifting in the wind.

After what felt like hours, he heard a movement behind him. He turned, his heart pounding in his ears. He now stood face-to-face with the sacred White Buffalo, and as he gazed into the bull's red eyes, he heard it speak.

"Ho, my *ceye*, I will be your spirit guide throughout your life. Walks with the Buffalo is what you will be called until the time you receive another. Go now, back to your people and tell them that you have been found worthy and your prayers have been heard."

In a blink, the vision was gone. His spirit veritably radiated hope, and he was filled with such excitement that he was no longer weak or thirsty. His heart was bubbling over with joy. His mind overwhelmed with wonderful thoughts. He had never, in all his wildest imaginings, thought for a moment that Wankan Tonka (the Great Spirit Buffalo) himself would hear his prayers let alone be his personal spirit guide.

Of all the things he had accomplished thus far in his short life, this was the most important. He had a new name and a new life.

He broke his fast that evening and as he lay beneath the wide expanse of sky, watching the spirit lights dancing among the campfires of his elders, he realized what he wanted to do with his life. Above all else, he wanted to be a healer of the people. He was already a hunter, protector and defender of his people. A warrior only when he had to be, since life was so precious to him. Searching his soul back then as he did now, he knew in his heart he would always keep his people first above all else, this was his pledge and prayer to the Great Spirit.

Young Thunder slept well that night, and the next morning as the sun rose, he offered his prayers of thanksgiving. But before leaving to return home, he picked up a piece of charcoal from the fire and decorated his war shield. He drew the image of the Great Buffalo upon it and ringed the outer edge with stars. This would forever be his symbol of power and protection. Not even the great Sitting Bull of the Sioux had one like it.

As he sat looking back on his life, Thunder realized that the boy of that day only saw the honor of such a great totem, however the man through the years had come to know the great heaviness of its responsibility and the sacrifices it had cost him. He remembered how as a boy, he had returned home, his heart light and filled with joy, only to later realize that as he related his tale around the counsel fire that it further set him apart from his peers. That young boy wanted so much to have friends and be accepted, but the Great Spirit had other plans for him. He was to become a man set apart.

Thunder Heart had become just that. He had closed off his heart after the death of Dancing Moon and women no longer held any interest for him. He filled his life instead with serving his people, learning everything he could about the healing arts, and helping his sister raise his son, Winter Blue, who he loved more than life itself.

CHAPTER 9: DESTINY CALLS

Now at the age of thirty, Thunder Heart sat again upon his high holy pinnacle praying and reflecting. He had accomplished so much in his life already; member of the Sacred Bowstrings, protected by the sacred White Buffalo, mighty hunter and warrior, Shaman, and healer. But there was something missing in his life and his spirit was very troubled. The dream that he was being plagued with was leaving his heart with deep feelings of loneliness, and this, the fourth night of his fast, was no exception.

After praying while staring into the flames of his campfire for most of the night, he finally drifted off to sleep, only to find himself once again immersed in the nightmare. He was lost in a sea of suffocating darkness fighting for air and chilled to the bone. After fighting the fear and blackness, for what seamed like an eternity, he finally awoke with a gasp. Sweat drenched his body and dripped from the tendrils of hair that hung from his forehead. He shook violently from cold chills even though his fire was hot and the weather warm. He had experienced such tribulations before. It was the emotional feeling of loss and despair that troubled him most. He couldn't shake the feeling that there was something he must do, or somewhere he had to go. Pulling his buffalo robe more snugly around his broad shoulders, he sat waiting for the sun rise.

Just before dawn, however, the wind picked up some, and though it was just the sound of the wind through the trees, Thunder could have sworn he heard a woman's cry for help. Lifting his arms and face skyward he cried out, "Great Spirit *Ma'heo'o*, please hear me! If the spirits will not take these dreams from me, show me what I must do, or where I must go to do your will! You have guided me all of my life! Please, I will trust you to guide me again, so that my spirit may once again find peace!"

So, with a troubled and lonely heart, he descended the mountain right after sunrise, his decision finally made. He would go on a long journey, letting the Buffalo Spirit guide him. During his ride down the mountain, he finalized his plans within his mind and rode right up to the lodge of his parents. Helee greeted her son with a quick hug and a smile, but she quickly realized from the look in his eyes that he had made a great decision. She knew in her mother's heart that he would be leaving. So, while her son sat eating and talking with the family, she packed his war bag and readied his horse. After dinner when he got up to leave, his family quickly hugged him and bid him farewell and safe journey.

Thunder Heart mounted his horse, thanked his mother, and rode out of the village holding his head high. He didn't know where he was headed, but he knew that the White Buffalo would lead him. Just as he cleared the village, Winter Blue came riding up along side of him calling out, "*A'te*, where are you going and when will you return?"

The boy was trying so hard to be a man, but Thunder Heart knew differently. He stopped his horse and nudged it closer to the boy's pinto mare.

"Blue, I must admit to you that I do not know. My spirit has been very troubled and I have asked the Great Spirit of the White Buffalo to guide me. I do not know when I will return, but I promise you I will."

The boy looked at his father and as tears welled in his eyes he asked,

"How will I know when you will return, *A'te*?"

Thunder Heart reaching out, patted his son on the shoulder and said, "Watch for the buffalo and look to Cha Ta. They will tell you. I am very proud of you my son. You are so much like our Uncle Beaver, and since you are such a fine warrior and provider, I ask that while I am away, that you would hunt and care for our Grandfather, Uncle Quiet waters. He is very wise in many things that a young man must know." Taking a hold of his son's arm, Thunder looked deeply into his deep, dark eyes. His voice suddenly cracking as he asked, "Will you do this for me, son?"

Blue, blinking back his tears, squared his shoulders, and placed a closed fist over his heart.

"*Va'Oht.* It is done, *A'te*! I swear it will be so."

Thunder Heart choked back his emotions and gave the boy a quick firm hug whispering in a trembling voice, "I love you too, my son. You have always made me proud, but now I must go. The spirit of the White Buffalo calls to me and I cannot rest until I have completed this quest."

Winter Blue nodded and turned his mount away to return to the village, but he rode only a short distance before he turned and shouted over his shoulder, "*Ne'me'hota'tse, A'te* (I love you, father)."

With hot, stinging tears sliding unbidden down his cheeks, Thunder Heart gave a quick wave of farewell before spurring his horse onward to disappear into the thick forest. He didn't want Blue to see the tears he could no longer keep from falling.

He was so proud of his son, and he understood why the boy made such an emotional parting gesture. Uncle Beaver had told the young warriors often that upon the day his own father rode off to fight the Blue Coats, he had not said what was in his heart, and he, to this day, regretted it. Thunder Heart knew that his son was afraid that he would never return, and so as he rode on, he let the tears fall to dry upon his face in the warm, sweet air of spring.

Thunder went off to find what was missing in his life. Perhaps he would find the spirit woman who was plaguing his dreams. She would call out to him from the midst of the storm with cries and screams so gut-wrenching at times that it jerked him awake, leaving him sweating and gasping in fear. Much as his father had done before him, he had spoken to Quiet Waters, the tribe's elder shaman, and accepted the fact that he had to find this woman now, and trust that the spirits would help him find what was missing in his life. Fearing he was losing his mind, he also knew that he wouldn't return home until his spirit was finally whole again.

At first he headed south, but for some reason, his way was continually blocked. After several days of fighting bad weather, rock falls, and wild animals, he finally turned westward. Once he found himself on the trail leading to Vancouver, his luck changed, and the traveling became uneventful.

Once the long trek over the mountain pass was completed, he descended into Dream Valley. This was the valley where his people had lived before the Great Fire had driven the whole tribe east to Mist Valley. After taking in the breathtaking beauty of Dream Valley, as his people called it, he made camp near the remains of his Uncle Black Crow's old, burned-out cabin. As he swept his eyes over the land, he was pleased to see that it was healing. The beaver had returned to the stream, the trees grew again, and the pasture grass was thick and high. Yes, this valley had healed nicely from the fire and again supported a multitude of wildlife.

Later that evening, sitting beside his fire and enjoying a roasted rabbit, he remembered the stories of the gold that was hidden under the floor of that cabin. Two prospectors had shot his father and left him for dead before traveling up river to Dream Valley where they violently raped two young maidens. The men were killed by his uncle Red Fox and their gold hidden. It was found that over the years that every spring, more gold would be found in the river only to also be hidden away to be used to buy supplies for the tribe. The next morning after deciding he had need of such wealth, he went in search of it. It took him many hours of digging but he finally found the charred leather pouch that contained two large palm-sized nuggets of pure gold as well as a draw string bag filled with smaller ones. He re-wrapped the heavy nuggets and placed them deep into his war bag. He would need spending money in the white man's world, and there were many things his people needed which he would bring them upon his return.

After reburying the smaller bag, he decided, since it was around noon and the day was quite warm, that he would go to the river to wash up and maybe do some fishing. As he walked through the fragrant meadow filled with wild flowers he could almost hear the voices of the past echoing back to him. The stories of long ago came to life in his mind. This was Dream Valley, the one that Ma'heo'o had lead his grandfather and his people to. Thunder Heart could see some of his people returning here to live one day soon. Mist Valley was becoming crowded, and while the hunting was good there, here was shelter from the severe winter winds, and there was large areas of flat land and terraces for planting crops.

The Cheyenne people had not wanted to change their way of life, but Helee, his mother, had taught them that they had to change to survive. And if they respected their mother, the Earth, she would continue to provide for her children. The people learned to build cabins and plant corn, squash, and beans, and bred and raised horses and dogs. They even worked with the loggers, showing them how to harvest the trees without stripping the land bare. The Mounties too had taught the men how to make sleds and teach their camp dogs to pull them so in the harsh winter it wouldn't take so long for a hunter to return home to his warm fire.

Thunder Heart thought about these things as he enjoyed the warm shallows of the small river that ran through the valley.

After bathing, he decided to fish, and while he sat there looking around, he could almost see a small town taking shape with a meeting house, trading post, saw mill, grist mill, school and a clinic. Smiling to himself, he realized that dreams came easy here in Dream Valley.

Later after eating the three fat trout he had caught, he rested under the star-filled sky. After only sleeping for a few hours, he was again thrust into the nightmare, but this time he saw the woman crying out for help as she was swept into the sea. He felt her body as it hit the frigid water, and gasped with her as the chill hit her flesh. It was so real that he awakened suddenly with a renewed sense of urgency. It was then that he decided he would put the nuggets value in cash into the bank in Vancouver to be used for all his people. With this decision made he left early the next day to continue riding along the westward trail.

CHAPTER 10: MARI LEAVES HOME

Mari sniffed back the tears as she packed her large trunk. It held all her memories: her childhood doll, her family Bible, and her mother's wedding dress. It also held all of her clothes. Her brother had sold their general store in Portland after their parents had died and said that they would start a new life for themselves in Vancouver, Canada. He said he had heard that it was a real up-and-booming place, and due to the access to the gold fields, they would soon become wealthy. No one there would know anything about their blood lines, which were rich with native heritage.

Mari had never been treated poorly in childhood, but her brother, Robert had been teased as a boy due to his dark skin, and it severely changed his life. They had called him Negro so much that he avoided going outside whenever possible, spending most of his time in the store with their father. In the summer, he still wore long sleeves and took up wearing a wide-brimmed straw hat to keep his skin from tanning as he ran the errands.

While she stood there staring into her trunk, haunted by memories, her brother walked into the room.

"Are you done yet? You know we have to be on that ship when the tide comes in. Besides, I want to get us a proper supper before we sail."

Mari chuckled, "Oh yes, I can see my green brute of a brother now hanging his head over the ship's railing. I, on the other hand, am looking forward to the smell of the salt spray and the wind in my hair. I want to stand at the bow of the ship and see if I can spot the whales."

Robert just shook his head. "Mari, the ever-fearless. Finish up now. The carriage is waiting." He returned outside.

She finished quickly, and after the trunks were loaded, she stood looking at the house for a moment. It had been her home since birth, as well as her grandparents' before that. She held the tears inside but one slid down her cheek and was whipped lovingly away by Robert as he lifted her into the carriage. Then he joined her. Taking her hands in his, he stated as the carriage pulled away, "I'm sorry, Sis. I didn't realize that leaving here would be so hard on you." Concern was written on his ruggedly handsome face.

"I didn't think it would be either, Robert, but so much of Momma and Papa are here that leaving just feels like losing them all over again."

As she noted the stricken look on his face, she pulled herself together for his sake and smiling, though sadly, she stated; "Look, Robert, endings are always hard, but what we are doing is right, and really, I am looking forward to our new beginning."

As the carriage rolled away down the street, she took a deep breath to steady herself before firmly setting her mind on the future. However, as she watched the familiar houses pass by, she again had to blink back tears as memories of old friends and her childhood assailed her mind. Before long, she stopped looking and started paying closer attention to Robert as he went on about his hopes and plans for the future. He rattled on about his vision of the new store, how and what he would stock it with. He even went on again about how the bankers had assured him that he was going to double his investment within the first year.

Smiling as she listened, she thought, making money. That was what excited her brother and gave him the courage to make this fearful sea voyage. She hoped that once his precious store was up and running that he would find a nice girl to love. He deserved to be happy in more ways than just making money.

She knew, even without seeing it, that they had reached the docks due to the overwhelming smell of fish that assailed her senses, making her gag. She didn't like fish very much, even though she did eat it at least once a week.

"There she is," her brother cried out excitedly and he hopped out of the carriage before it could come to a complete stop. When he opened the door for Mari to get out, she was awed by the sight of the large schooner.

The Anna Bella Lee was far from new, but you would never have known that just by looking. Her decks were highly polished, her brass shone and glinted in the sun, her sails and rigging were firm and in good repair and her crew were clean and sober.

Robert helped her down from the carriage, and after he instructed the mate to take their trunks to their cabin, they headed to a restaurant just down the street.

The Sea Shore Hotel and Restaurant was a large green building with yellow shutters. Inside, it held accommodations and dining for fifty as well as a bar with gaming tables in the back. What impressed Mari the most was the fine linen table clothes on each table and the lace curtains on the windows, as well as the fresh cut flowers on each table.

They were escorted to a table by the window and Mari noticed while they were seated that the flowers masked the wharf smell to a great degree. Taking a deep whiff, she secretly thanked God for them because she could not have eaten a thing otherwise.

Once seated, a young woman in a bright yellow dress wearing a white starched apron took their order, and while they waited for their food, Mari stared at the opulence while Robert went to the bar for a quick drink. She guessed it was to steady his nerves.

When their food came, she ate hers gingerly as Robert wolfed his down like he hadn't eaten in a week of Sundays. She just shook her head, silently thinking he would just heave it up later anyway.

When they were finished, Robert paid for the meals, leaving a generous tip for the waitress, and they left strolling arm-in-arm down the board walk, stopping only briefly to buy some peppermint sticks for the voyage.

When they arrived at the gangplank, they were met by the ship's Captain and First Mate who introduced themselves as Captain Clancy and Mr. Martin.

"Welcome aboard Mr. and Miss Fairweather. The mate on board will show you to your cabin."

Robert walked up the gangplank with ease, but just as she reached the halfway point, a sudden swell caused her to lose her balance. She would have ended up in the drink if not for the quick reflexes of Mr.

Martin.

He had quickly snaked an arm around her waist and drew her to his firm body.

Mari turned crimson red from the top of her head to the tip of her toes, and she thought she would faint from embarrassment before she made it on board ship. Once her feet were firmly on the deck, Mr. Martin released her, quickly taking off his hat and begged her pardon.

Smiling broadly, he asked, "Miss Fairweather, after we get underway, would you accompany me for a stroll on deck?"

Mari smiled shyly, and through lowered lashes stated, "I would be pleased sir. I was hoping to spot some whales up close."

Robert laughed to himself at his sister's antics as she animatedly chattered to the Mate all the way to their cabin. Once inside, he settled in to the cabin by stretching his long frame onto his bunk with a book in his hand.

"Do you wish to rest, Sis? Or would you like me to read to you? I have a new book. It's called *Moby Dick*. It's about whales and the sea."

"Oh, Robert, please do. It sounds wonderful."

So, just as they did at home, Robert read to her while her mind painted pictures of the story in her mind. It took several hours to get the ship under full sail, but true to his word, Martin came and escorted Mari to the main deck for a stroll. Martin was such a gentleman, just the kind of man she had dreamed of, and she was quite smitten with him. As they walked around the ship, he told her of his life at sea and answered every question she asked about the ship, the sea life, and what to expect on the voyage. But what Mari liked best was when they stood on the bow of the ship where she could feel the vessel rise and fall with each wave, the sea spray on her face, and the wind in her hair. Martin held onto Mari and was completely smitten by her beauty and the way her joy bubbled forth from her in tinkling laughter. They stood there watching for whales until the ship's bell signaled that it was time for supper.

Martin escorted Mari to the Captain's dining room where she found her brother already engrossed in a conversation about trade goods with the Captain. Martin helped her to be seated, and while the meal was a simple one of chicken, potatoes, and biscuits, Mari marveled at the ingenious ways they had of keeping the lights and dishes in place as the ship rocked to and fro.

After the meal, Martin escorted them back to their cabin, but before Martin let go of her hand he bowed and placed a kiss on it. Mari blushed so deeply that she felt her cheeks turn hot and her knees go weak. Leaning heavily on her cabin door, she almost couldn't catch her breath, but finally, as she gazed into Martin's green eyes, she managed a shy smile. Martin, realizing the affect he had had on her and loving it, smiled broadly.

"Good night, Miss Mari. Sleep well."

Finally finding her voice she squeaked out, "Good night to you too, Mr. Martin."

Entering the cabin, Mari knew she would not find sleeping this night easy. A man, a very handsome man, had kissed her hand.

She touched her lips and tried to imagine what it would feel like to be really kissed. She shuddered and her lips tingled, parting slightly.

"Hey, what's the matter with you?" interjected Robert with a chuckle in his voice. "You sick or something?"

Startled and suddenly embarrassed all over again, she cried out, "Oh, you. It's none of your business. And no, I am not sick. I had a wonderful time. Martin was a perfect gentleman. Now, pull your bed curtains. I wish to get ready for bed."

"Okay, your majesty. Do you want me to read to you some more, Sis? You look like you might need something to focus on to help you fall asleep."

Sighing heavily, she said, "Thank you, Robert. I think you may be right."

Mari undressed quickly, and after pulling on her night rail, she slipped under the thick blankets to settle warmly into the feather mattress. Robert drew back his curtains and started reading again, but soon realized that Mari was fast sleep. He marked her page but continued to read on silently.

After about three hours, Robert was awakened by a scream. Mari was thrashing wildly in her bed, sweat pouring like water from her face. She was gasping for breath and reaching out for something only she could see. Robert called out to her but it had no effect.

Finally, he got out of bed, and taking hold of her shoulders, shook her, saying firmly, "Mari, Mari wake up. Wake up, I say!"

When she finally came back to the real world and realized that Robert was holding her, she threw her arms around him and started weeping.

"Oh, Robert, it was so horrible. I dreamed there was a horrible storm and we crashed into the rocks. I was sinking beneath the cold water and I couldn't breathe. Oh, oh, it was so real. Don't let go, Robert. Don't ever let me go. Please!"

Brushing the hair from her face, Robert held Mari tightly, rocking her back and forth as if she were a child again. Mari, his poor Mari. He had uprooted her and placed her on this boat just to follow his dreams. He hadn't realized until now how frightening all this had been for her and he was suddenly filled with guilt.

When Mari finished composing herself she asked, "This dream, Robert. What does it mean?"

"It means nothing, Sis. Except that you ate a heavy meal and my book over-stimulated your imagination. Now go back to sleep, dear. I will keep the small lamp burning for you."

Mari had calmed down a lot after telling Robert about her dream, so much so that she even tried to smile when he placed a kiss on her forehead, but the dream had felt so real; too real. She still felt chilled from the experience, and pulled the blankets higher over her slender shoulders. She now wished their trip was over, her excitement replaced by a sickening sense of foreboding.

The next morning dawned with a reddish glow in the east, and even though it was gloriously beautiful to behold, there was a place in the back of Mari's mind that felt unnerved. As the sun rose higher and the stars winked out one by one, Mari put the nagging feelings out of her mind. The air was calm, and there wasn't a cloud in the sky. Mr. Martin found her standing by the main mast, listening to one of the sailors playing a waltz on an old French squeeze box. With eyes twinkling, Martin bowed before her, sweeping his hat off and out to the side in a most grand fashion.

Mari unsuccessfully stifled a girlish giggle as he rose with a roguish grin on his handsome face. "Miss Mari. May I have this dance?"

Never having been asked to dance before, Mari blushed and held out her small hand. "Why yes, kind sir. I would be delighted." Martin, taking her hand, swept her into his arms. Holding her firmly around the waist, he gazed deeply into her eyes as he swirled her around the deck.

"Miss Mari, the wind has been strong and at our backs all day. We should be in port by morning tomorrow, and I was wondering if I could visit you. I would love nothing more than to get to know you better."

Mari blushed again and lowering her eyes stated, "If it's alright with my brother. I would like that very much."

They continued to dance until Captain Clancy came out of his cabin and commanded Martin to take the bridge.

Mari, now winded from dancing and fatigued from her lack of sleep the night before, returned to her cabin and decided to take a nap. She awoke much later to the sound of a sailor pounding on the door.

Robert answered it only to have a food tray shoved into his arms before the man hurriedly stated, "Sorry folks. No time for formal meals. There's a bad storm coming in. The Captain says you folks need to stay in your cabin till it passes."

Fear settled in a hard cold lump in the pit of Mari's stomach and her chin began to tremble. Robert set down the tray and took her into his strong arms and calmly reassured her before planting a kiss on her forehead.

"Come now, Sis, the cook has sent you some tea. Sit, hun, and eat something now. I'm afraid if the ship starts heaving, so will we." She nodded and poured them each a cup of tea. As she sipped the strong brew, a cold fear grew so big within her that even the hot drink couldn't dispel it.

Something bad was coming.

CHAPTER 11: SERGEANT O'MALLEY

Sergeant William O'Malley sat at his desk in the Vancouver's Mounted Polices office building, looking out the window at the bustling street.

During his career as a Canadian Mountie, he had seen Vancouver grow from a village, to a town, and then into a city. He really disliked the fast-paced life of the city, and he longed for the open country again. He loved riding the circuit with his old friend and mentor, Erin O'Toole, and the country's Indians and their lifestyle. When his old friend died, he had purchased his predecessor's cabin to retire in, but even that wasn't as far as he wanted to escape to. Sergeant O'Toole had been killed shortly after he had retired. William missed his old friend, and was deeply saddened that he hadn't gotten to enjoy his retirement.

Will's life had been ruled by the service, and he had never married. It wasn't that he didn't want to, but few women could tolerate his months away from home while he rode his circuit. He thought of his friends in Mist Valley, and wished he could settle there with them. He felt that if too many white men settled there, he would not be welcomed, or even safe, but he knew that Dream Valley was ripe again for settlement. He felt that with all he knew about engineering, he could help the people there to build their own grist mill and even a saw mill. He could teach them to farm the valley, and with this added food source they could feed their people better and protect their lands from being over-hunted, and thus sustain a healthier population that was self-sustaining, as well as protected from the outside world.

Smiling to himself, he turned away from the window, picked up a pencil and paper from his desk, and started to make a list of the things he would need to take with him if he got permission to settle in Dream Valley. Such things as: a plow, an anvil, basic blacksmith tools, a large band saw, engineering and farming books, etc. All he had to do was figure out how to pay for everything and obtain permission from the tribe to settle there.

Suddenly, his peaceful dreaming was interrupted. He let out a deep sigh. Life and reality beckoned again, so he shoved the pad with its list of dreams back into his desk drawer and followed his clerk out of his office to settle some kind of pressing matter of the day.

Sergeant William O'Malley was a stubborn man however, and all the trouble in the world could not stop him from dreaming. He hoped he would live long enough for his superiors to accept his request for early retirement.

When he came out of his office he was met by the town sheriff.

"Mornin' Sergeant. I want to make you aware of a disturbing matter I've encountered with the Indians around these parts."

"Oh, and what might that be, Sir?" asked O'Malley.

"Well, there have been a series of deadly accidents where Indian logging workers have been killed. I figured that seeing how you are on good terms with them, you could get a handle on things out there before they start killing whites too."

O'Malleys eyes narrowed and his blood began to boil. He disliked the small sheriff, but now he wanted nothing more than to punch him in his bigoted face. "So, you think the ones doin' the killin' are Indians? And what gave you that idea?"

"I have the testimony of several loggers," stated the Sheriff. "A one Mister Radner said that he saw Blue Hawk set the trap, but it got triggered early and another Indian was killed instead. Just wanted to let you know that we arrested Blue Hawk and he is behind bars awaiting hanging."

Sergeant O'Malley was burning inside with rage. He knew Blue Hawk was a drunk, but he didn't think him a cowardly killer. So, through gritted teeth, he bid the sheriff good day and turned to his clerk.

"I be needin' ya to do some runnin' for me today, laddy."

Standing at attention, the young man stated, "Yes, sir. Whatever your need, sir. Do you think you can help Mr. Blue Hawk, sir?"

"I dunno, Mr. Scott, but we'll try. The tribes know ye, so I want ye to ride out and talk to the Indian loggers and bring me back their reports as quick as possible. I would also like ye to tell Mr. Eastfield I want him to pretend to be a logger and hire on with the same outfit that this Radner fella is with. Tell him to keep his ears open and watch his back. I got a feelin' this Radner is a filthy polecat."

"Yes, sir, I'll get right on it, sir," the clerk said as he left the office at an almost dead run.

William just shook his head and said to himself as he returned to his paper work, "I need a drink. Somethin's not right up there on the mountain, and my bones hurt. There must be a storm a'comin', I think."

After pouring himself a cup of scotch, Sergeant O'Malley leaned back in his chair, put his feet upon his desk, and savored the smooth whiskey as it warmed his tired bones and went back to dreaming.

CHAPTER 12: CITY BY THE SEA

Thunder Heart would have liked to enjoy the peacefulness of his trip, but the dreams drove him onward like a mad man. The farther west he rode, the stormy nightmares became more vivid and harder to put out of his mind.

One night, after he had been on the road for weeks, he awakened in a dead fright with sweat trickling down his ashen face and gasping for breath. He had seen her so clearly this time— Lord, he had even *been* her— as she was swept from the deck of a great sailing ship into the churning, heaving, frigid sea. His spirit struggled along with hers as she was tossed and dragged deep within the waves, feeling her lungs burning for breath. He experienced what it felt like to give up to the cold as she lay alone and forgotten on a barren stretch of rocky beach.

After composing himself enough to stand, he rapidly broke camp. It wasn't even dawn yet when he mounted his horse and began riding hard on the well-worn trail leading to the great city on the western coast: Vancouver. Though the Spirits were compelling him to hurry, he knew there was still time to find the woman, as the air was dry and the clouds were only wisps high in the sky.

With deep faith he allowed the dreams to push him onward often riding through the night, dozing on and off in the saddle. Despite this, it still took him a full week to complete his journey.

Then one morning, he sat atop a rise overlooking the beautiful city of the western coast. From this distance, one couldn't see her dirtier, seedier side. All that could be seen from here were beautiful houses nestled among flowering trees, huge stone buildings, and tall ships anchored in a peaceful harbor. Thunder was amazed at the sight, and while he was anxious about being among so many whites, he was also relieved because he saw no evidence of any destruction from a great storm yet.

Spurring his horse onward, he held his posture erect and held his head high as he rode straight down Main Street. He took no offense to the looks, sneers, and cat calls he was given by the people he passed. He knew that Indians were not well-liked here, so he headed right to the Mounties' head office, which he found easily due to its bright flag that flew proudly before it.

Dismounting and tying his pony to the rail, he ignored the stares of the curious passersby and walked right inside the two-story, whitewashed building.

Once inside, he met a wide-eyed young clerk who stammered out, "Sergeant, sergeant! There's an Indian in here!"

"Well, me boy, ask the man why he's here," came the sergeant's reply.

Thunder Heart, recognizing the sergeant's voice, stated loudly with a broad smile on his face, "I've come to see you, Uncle O'Malley."

The Sergeant hurried out of his office to greet Thunder Heart with open arms and a huge bear hug. Sergeant O'Malley was a tall, big-boned Irishman with a broad smile, a handle bar mustache, and a commanding disposition. He had known Thunder's family since he was a child, and had traveled the long circuit through the mountains so often that he brought trade goods to the tribe almost on a yearly basis. He was not as spry as he once had been, and now being over fifty, he was looking forward to retirement. He stayed close to home and office nowadays, allowing the younger men to do the extensive traveling.

"Thunder, me boy," he said in his heavy Irish brogue. "Tis good to see ya. Come now into me office and tell me everything. How's yer folks, and what brings ya all this way, lad?" Sergeant O'Malley clasped a big, beefy arm around Thunder's broad shoulders and led him back to his office, leaving a very puzzled clerk behind at his desk.

Once in the office, Thunder set down his heavy war bag, took a seat in the oak arm chair that sat before the sergeant's desk, and informed his friend of his need to exchange some gold for supplies. He didn't tell Sergeant O'Malley of his dreams however, but instead asked if he knew of a cabin not far from the bay where he could stay and hunt for a while.

The sergeant rose from where he sat on his desk, clapped the young man in buckskins on the back and said, "Sure I do, me boy." Then he turned and walked over to the book shelf where he obtained a small mahogany box. Upon opening it, he retrieved a large brass key and handed it to Thunder Heart. "This be the key to me own cabin, laddy. I'll not be a needin' it for a while. Tis well stocked and resides well within the Indian reserve. It be peaceful and quiet there and no one will be a bother to ye there."

Thunder was overcome. "Thank you, Uncle. I am truly in your debt."

"Nah, me boy. Yer not. Yer family and ye would do the same fir me. Now have a wee bit of coffee with me, lad." He handed Thunder a cup of steaming brew. "Sit fir awhile, me boy, and tell me everything. I have missed yer ma a great deal, ya know."

Thunder Heart and the sergeant visited for quite a while over several cups of coffee. He filled the sergeant in on everything that had happened with the tribe since his last visit. Then after thanking his friend, he left to go to the bank, but changed his mind and returned to the Mounties' office. He was afraid that the banker might be tempted to cheat him, so he asked the sergeant to go with him.

The bank was a large stone building that sat next to the general store just down the street from the Mounties' office. It was all polished wood and marble and made a hollow sound when you walked inside. Thunder had been right to bring the Mountie with him, because the teller eyed him with disdain as he walked up to him.

"State yer business, injun," the teller sneered. He gave Thunder no more resistance when Sergeant O'Malley cleared his throat and stated that Thunder was with him and that the boy's family had an account there. Thunder thought the teller's eyes would pop out of his head when he hefted the large nuggets up onto the counter and stated, using very good English, that he wanted the nuggets appraised and their worth in current market value placed into the Hawk family account.

Upon seeing the smile of avarice spreading across the teller's face, Thunder commanded firmly, "Do not try to cheat me, sir. I am well educated and I will tell my uncle, here…" He pointed to Sergeant O'Malley. "…If you ever do so."

The teller then nodded his understanding and took the rocks to the scales. Upon quick appraisal of the almost pure nuggets weighing close to fifty pounds each, it changed the banker's whole demeanor. The teller quickly figured the value, and while smiling broadly, wrote the sum on a piece of paper and handed it to Thunder asking, "Is there anything else I may do for you, sir?"

Thunder was amazed at his wealth, and the respect that this wealth afforded him. The nuggets were placed into the safe and their worth recorded in the banks permanent records. Sergeant O'Malley witnessed it and Thunder was immediately given a line of credit in the form of a note from the bank's president to be given to the neighboring store keeper, enabling him to purchase all he or his people would ever need.

He bid the Sergeant goodbye as he entered the general store, and when he approached the store keeper he was astounded by the gentleman's friendliness.

"Well, young man, the name's Ike Jones. What can I help you with this fine day?"

Thunder liked this large, rotund man with twinkling eyes, so he offered him his hand to see if he would accept it. He approached the counter, hand extended, and when Thunder's hand was grasped firmly, he stated, "Thank you, sir. My name is Thunder Heart and I am in need of just a few things for now, but later I will be taking a lot of things back to my people."

It was then that he handed the man the letter from the bank, and the storekeeper studied it only briefly before placing it into his drawer. Taking out his ledger, he opened it to a new page and had Thunder sign it.

"Well, Thunder Heart, I'm really glad to be doing business with you and your people. Gather up what you need for right now and as soon as you know what your people will need, give me a list and I'll set aside the items for you, and if I don't have what you need or not enough of what you need, I'll order it. I can have most things here in as quickly as a week."

"Thank you, Mr. Jones," replied Thunder. "That is very helpful to know."

But if I may be so bold, can I ask, considering the way Indians are disliked around here, is it only my money that motivates your kindness or is there another reason, sir?"

"Well, young man I do like the money and the business, but I treat all men the same, because my God is no respecter of persons. Besides, my grandfather came out here when only the Indians lived here and built this business. I wouldn't even have this store if it weren't for them and the trade my grandfather built with them."

"Well, Mr. Jones, I am truly pleased to meet such an honorable man and you will definitely be getting all my business from now on."

Thunder walked around the well-stocked store gathering up all the items he needed, and Ike started a book for him, keeping an accurate record of the tally for the banker.

Thunder Heart loved the feel of his buckskins, but he realized he should try to blend in more from time to time, so he purchased a couple of soft whip cord pants and two plaid logger's shirts.

The store keeper wrapped every item and placed them in cotton bags. Smiling, Ike shook Thunder's hand again before he left and bid him good hunting and asked him to come again.

Upon leaving the store, Thunder was hit with that unsettling sense of urgency again. With his heart pounding and gooseflesh dancing on his arms, he quickly tied his purchases to his horse, mounted up, and rode straight for O'Malley's cabin.

As he rode, he could see the dark clouds gathering off into the distance and feel the wind beginning to pick up. Overwhelmed with this need to reach this spiritual appointment, he pushed his horse to go faster and soon the pounding of the hoof beats matched the pounding within his chest.

Ike Jones hadn't seen the short, dirty, bearded logger until he came up to the counter holding a tin of chewing tobacco.

"May I help you, fella?" Ike asked.

"Yea, I needs me some tabackie. How much?"

Ike could hardly stand the man's smell. It was turning his stomach, but a customer was a customer, so he replied, "That will be two bits, cash only."

The logger bristled. "Hey, I didn't see that injun pay ya in cash."

Ike took the logger's bait and became so angry he blurted out, "For your information, that injun paid with a bank note. Hell, his family has enough money that they could buy this whole town if they had a mind to. Now do you want that tobacco or not?"

"Yea, give me a spell. Don't get your bloomers in a bunch. I gots it right here." The logger tossed the bits of gold onto the counter, but before he left, he asked, "How you suppose an injun got so gall-darn rich anyways?"

Hearing this, Ike lost it. "Hell if I know. Maybe they struck gold or something. Now be off with ya. I got work to do."

The logger left, and Ike was glad that the smelly old fart was gone. As he went back to stocking his shelves, he pondered about the young Indian himself; not how rich he was, but how he had learned to read and write.

After riding through the pristine forest for over an hour and a half, Thunder finally saw the cabin. It was a small but sturdy structure, set back from the sea high upon a bluff surrounded by old growth trees and covered with moss and vines. He quickly unpacked his stores and stabled his tired mount behind the cabin under the lean to back porch.

This addition was a very practical way to protect the stock as well as keep large quantities of firewood stacked dry and handy. The cabin's warm log walls kept the animals warm enough on cool nights, but when the weather became extremely bitter, small squares of the logs could be pulled out of the cabins wall allowing warmth to flood the porch, which could be insulated by stacking bales of straw on two sides and placing a buffalo hide over the third for a door. The livestock could then feed off the bales, thus giving rise to the comical saying of eating oneself out of house and home.

Thunder Heart slipped the large brass skeleton key into the door's lock and with a click and a squeak, the heavy wooden door swung open. The cabin was sparsely decorated, yet well-organized, but it was cold and smelled of dirt and dampness. He carried in his bags of supplies and his buffalo robe and put them away before quickly laying a fire. Still filled with restlessness, he picked up a homemade straw broom and set about cleaning up the place, ridding it of months of dust, spiders, and cobwebs. Once this was done he took up his bow and went hunting. He had just returned to the cozy, warm dwelling with three rabbits and a small turkey when the storm hit.

With each crash of thunder, his anxiety increased and his heart threatened to race away. He kept his mind busy by roasting one of the rabbits for his supper and brewed himself a calming mint tea. He dressed out the other two hares and gutted and hung the fowl. By the time this was done he sat calmly beside the fire eating and reading one of the many books he had found in the cabin. The one on the healing arts he found was most informative. As the storm outside began to rage, he could hear the trees wailing and flailing in the forceful wind, so he began to pray. Rocking and chanting, he sat cross-legged upon his white buffalo robe before the warm glowing fire and prayed that *Ma'heo'o's* will be done in all things.

Thunder Heart had dreams of warning all his life and they disturbed him greatly, but after so many years, he had finally accepted them as a sacred burden. This gift of knowing what was to come carried with it great responsibilities. Often in the past, his only responsibility was to pass on the information and let others do what must be done, but this time, the burden of life and death was his alone. His mother, when he told her of his recent dreams, had smiled and looked deep into her son's eyes and told him that the woman and he shared a common destiny, and like when his father followed his dreams and had sought her, he must seek this storm woman and see how their lives were connected.

And so, he was here waiting in a cabin by the sea, but waiting was becoming difficult. He got up and started rummaging through the cabinets. He found some canned goods, some assorted pots and pans, and an old bottle of whiskey. He didn't like the alcohol of the white man, but he had to still the pounding of his heart. He poured some into his tea and began reading again until he drifted off into a restless sleep.

CHAPTER 13: THE STORM

The storm hit with the force of a hurricane in the middle of the night just as the frigate reached the mouth of the harbor. The huge waves and gale force winds tossed the sailing vessel like a toy. The Captain was trying frantically to head the ship back out to sea, but suddenly, while being pelted with hail and driving rain, the main mast twisted, and with a sickening crack it snapped and came crashing down to the deck below.

Screaming orders to his crew, Captain Clancy tied himself to the ship's wheel. He would steer the ship with his last ounce of strength, heading it now into the harbor in an attempt to get it close enough to land so his crew could abandon ship. The crew with safety ropes tied to their waists worked with all their strength to bring in the sails, but their efforts were hindered by the huge swells that crashed and pounded the vessel. Any crew that ventured out without a safety rope was swept overboard. Seeing that the ship was headed for the rocks, the Captain gave the order to abandon ship and prayed that they would have the time needed before the ship broke apart.

Mari laid in her bunk below deck, listening to the screaming of the wind, unable even to dress due to the severe tossing of the ship. Suddenly, there came a pounding on the cabin door. It was Martin, the first mate. "Mari, Mari and Robert, get up!" He screamed. "Now!" When they didn't open the door right away, Martin kicked it in. Holding onto the door frame and then the bunk, he yanked the fear-paralyzed Mari to her feet. Her voice trembling as she clung to him for support, she yammered "My God, Martin, what's happening?!"

"We have to abandon ship, Robert," said the Captain. "I want Mari to hold onto me and we'll get to a life boat, okay?"

Hysterical, Mari screamed "I can't, Robert. I can't!"

Robert took hold of her shoulders and shook her, but when that didn't stop her hysterics, he slapped her. He hated to do it, but she meant the world to him and he would protect her even if he had to knock her out to do it.

"Mari, SHUT UP and hang onto Martin. Now, let's go, NOW!"

Hanging onto each other, they made their way to the forward ladder, banging from side-to-side down the hall as they went. She headed up the ladder first, with Robert behind to keep her from falling off, but once they reached the hatch, Robert and Martin had to pass her and use all of their strength to lift the heavy door. Once the hatch was open, the rain and seawater poured over them, its cold sapping their strength immediately. Just as Mari reached up for Martin to help her onto the deck, a mighty wave crashed over the ship and washed her back down the ladder. Martin jumped back below deck and fought his way through the water to rescue her and bring her up the ladder. Once again on the main deck, Martin ushered them into the Captain's cabin. They weren't there very long before the secondary mast snapped and came crashing down, smashing the cabin and pinning Mari and Robert under the debris. With the help of the waves, Martin freed them and left them clinging with the help of ropes to the ship's rails as the crew made ready the lifeboat.

Mari and Robert, however, didn't realize that in a storm this strong, the driving winds and huge waves, as well as the torrents of falling rain, would sink a ship this size in a very short time.

They waited, clinging with draining strength to the railing. Mari, feeling her hand slipping as a wave washed over the deck, entwined her hand in the rope that was tied to the rail. Robert held onto Mari as well as the wave-battered railing, but upon seeing the ship's young cabin boy about to be swept into the sea, he leapt out to save his life, leaving his sister behind. Mari screamed, "Robert No!" as a giant wave washed him and the boy from her sight. Mari continued to cling to the railing until another giant wave smashed the vessel into the rocks busting the railing and flinging both her and it into the frigid, churning sea.

The water engulfed her at once, pulling her downward. She held her breath until her lungs burned, and she gasped for air as she bobbed back to the surface. Coughing and choking, swallowing a mouth full of seawater, she pulled her shivering body up onto the broken railing that by some miracle she had remained entangled with.

Grateful for this fragile hold on life, Mari prayed. She prayed for her brother, who gave his life to safe the boy, and the lives of the ship's crew, and each time a wave pulled her under, only to bob back to the surface again, she prayed and said thank you.

After what felt like an eternity, and feeling her remaining strength leaving her, she entangled her arms and legs further with the railing, and then saying a last prayer for her own life, she relaxed and let the sea take her.

CHAPTER 14: RESCUED

Suddenly, Thunder Heart was awakened to the sound of a woman's scream and a distant cry for help. With his heart thundering within his chest and a prayer on his lips, he wrapped a blanket around his waist and threw a slicker over his head. Unused to a hat, but needing one to keep the rain out of his eyes, he donned one of the Mounties' hats and ran outside.

The rain fell in swift torrents, often horizontally as it was driven by the strong winds coming off of the ocean. Even though the narrow trail down to the sea was muddy and slick, Thunder Heart made the beach in record time. The rain was making it hard to see very far ahead, but he headed toward the crashing waves and some washing debris that he had seen. It was then that he heard a weak, pitiful cry for help.

Thunder Heart flew into an all-out run then, just reaching the woman and pulling her from the waves as they were about to drag her again out to sea. Untangling her from the railing upon which she was bound, he dragged her higher upon the beach before turning her over and feeling for the pulse at her neck. Relieved that she was still alive, he swept the wet hair from her face. Upon seeing her, his breath caught in his throat and he began to tremble inside. She was the woman from his dreams.

She was angelically beautiful, small-boned and frail, but her lips were so blue, causing the healer in him to fly into action. He took off the blanket he wore and quickly wrapped her within it before carefully scooping her up to hold her next to his warm body under the rain slicker. Traversing the path to the cabin was harder going up than down, but soon they were both within the safety of the cabin.

He laid the unconscious woman by the fire and quickly stripped off his wet and dirty clothes. Then he did the same for the woman. She was so cold and blue, but she was not Dancing Moon, and he knew now what to do to save her. He threw several logs on the fire and began to rub her arms and legs vigorously. He had to get her circulation going again. He quickly bathed her in warm water while he checked her for injuries. Then he took a soft towel and dried her hair and body. He knew she should not be warmed too quickly or covered too tightly until the color of her skin was even. This would show that her circulation was returning to normal again.

As he looked upon her, he sighed deeply and gritted his teeth. He would have to take off all his clothes and rest with her under the dry blankets. This was the best way to warm her, but she made manly feelings flood his mind. The least of which was a possessive protectiveness and a healer's concern for her health.

Pulling her close to his naked, warm body, she let out a small sigh, and Thunder Heart had to use all of his inner strength to keep his body under control. She felt so good in his embrace, so soft, yet well-muscled, and she fit so well in his arms, as if she were made just for him. After a while, he finally fell asleep, safe in the knowledge that his charge was now within his care.

That next day and night was hard for Thunder Heart. Though her circulation had improved enough for him to dress, Mari remained in a shock-induced sleep, tossing and turning, often crying out, as if in pain. He tried to spoon-feed her some tea, and he couldn't get much down her throat, yet it was enough to help her rest more comfortably.

Once Thunder Heart thought she had warmed sufficiently by the fire, he dressed her in one of his soft flannel shirts and moved her to the bed. He stood there gazing down on her beautiful form for a long time. He couldn't help himself; he reached out and brushed a strand of hair from her face. He caressed her cheek with the back of his fingers and let out a deep sigh as he pulled blankets over her, tucking them under her small chin.

He shook his head and mentally asked, *Why Ma'heo'o? Why a white woman? What have I done that you should bring this upon me?*

As he settled himself by the fire so he could keep it going throughout the night, it dawned him that he was glad that he had saved her. Thunder was mentally and physically exhausted, and as soon as he got comfortable, he fell asleep.

Deep in the night however, the wind picked up again, howling through the trees like a mournful old woman. Suddenly, a tree limb snapped and hit against the house, causing Mari to bolt upright in bed and scream out, "Robert, no!"

Thunder Heart jolted awake, rushed to the bed and gathered her up into his arms, holding her as if she were a babe. She clung to him, trembling like a leaf, and placing her head on his chest over his thundering heart, she soaked his shirt with her tears. Caressing her softly, he ran his hand over her thick auburn hair and whispered soft words to her in Cheyenne. After she calmed down, he tried to lay her back down upon the bed, but she continued to cling to him so tightly that he decided to remain on the bed with her. So, there he sat, up against the wall, cradling her within his powerful arms while she slept.

Unable to go back to sleep in this position, he found himself studying her features. She was slender, yet muscular, with soft, rounded curves and hips just wide enough to bare many children. Her breasts were high and firm with nipples that hardened at his slightest touch. Her hair was a deep auburn that danced with gold highlights in the firelight. Her face was like an angel's with full perfectly-shaped lips, eyes framed with thick, dark lashes, and delicate, soft brown brows. He realized that he had lain naked with her that first night, totally focused on her survival, but now he looked upon her not as a patient, but as a woman. He found himself overcome with emotions he thought long since dead, and his body responded to her nearness. Thunder's feelings warred within him. He had sworn to *Ma'heo'o* that he would take no other woman, but here she was so beautiful, so alone and needy. He silently raged with himself, but deep inside him, he heard the Spirit Buffalo whisper, "She is the one."

Unable to release her, and feeling the overwhelming need to caress her, he picked up the hairbrush from off the nightstand and started brushing her hair. He was well-pleased with himself when she smiled and relaxed, and he found he enjoyed doing this task while she rested with her head now in his lap. However, it didn't take long before she wiggled her head a little too much, and his arousal became too much for him to bear. He parted from her then, laying her ever-so-gently back on the bunk.

Disgusted with his body, he went outside to get some more wood for the fire. He didn't want a woman in his life, but the more he thought about her beautiful, young body, the harder he became. Finally, he headed to the outhouse to take the situation in hand. Literally. After about fifteen minutes, he went back inside to build up the fire again and cook some breakfast.

CHAPTER 15: AT THE CABIN

Mari awoke the next morning, wide-eyed and fearful. However, she didn't cry out, but silently scanned the sparse interior of the small, one room cabin. When her eyes came to rest on the wide expanse of Thunder Heart's bare shoulders, her eyes widened with surprise. He was deeply tanned and had thick, long, straight hair that hung almost to his waist. She admired the color of it as it danced in the firelight, and she compared it to the color of a raven's wing in the sun light. She watched for quite awhile, admiring the way his lean muscles rippled powerfully beneath his bronzed skin. For some reason unknown to her, her body flushed as she watched him, and warmth spread within her, settling deep in her belly.

As she considered her situation, she thought, *I should be afraid, but for some reason I'm not.*

Slowly rising up in bed, holding the blanket tight to her bosom, she addressed the handsome stranger.

"Hello, kind sir. Thank you for helping me, but... where am I?"

Thunder Heart's heart leapt with excitement at the sound of her sweet voice, but he rose and turned slowly. That's when his eyes met the most beautiful pair of blue eyes he had ever imagined. They were a perfect crystal blue, like the sky at first light. They stared at each other for a moment, then smiling softly, he approached, slowly handing her a cup of tea. Fearful of how she would react to his Indian heritage, Thunder made a quick decision and took the first name of John.

"Hello, miss. I am John Thunder Heart, and this cabin belongs to a friend of mine, Sergeant O'Malley of the Canadian Mounted Police. I heard you call out for help and found you on the shore amongst the debris of a shipwreck."

Her eyes suddenly turned sad, and with a trembling voice, she asked. "Did you find anyone else?"

"I'm sorry. I didn't find anyone else nearby. You were so cold that I feared for your life, so I brought you here with great haste."

He approached her slowly and knelt down by the bed. She noticed how his buckskin pants stretched taught around his thighs, and she blushed with embarrassment as he handed her a cup of wonderful-smelling liquid.

"Here now. Drink this tea while I get your clothing for you. I've sweetened it with honey to give you strength."

She reached up with trembling fingers to take the cup and glanced quickly at his eyes. Upon seeing his face, she blushed, again, to the very roots of her hair, at the thought of this handsome stranger with dark eyes having seen her naked.

Thunder Heart smiled softly with understanding as he reached down and caressed her cheek, moving a stray lock of her silky beautiful hair as he did so.

"Do not worry small one," he said. "I am a healer, and I only did what I had to do to save your life. Nothing more. When you are stronger, we will go into the town and ask if there are any others who survived the storm. What is your name? I can't continue to call you Small One."

Mari blushed, again, and after taking a long drink of tea, she smiled and said, "My name is Mari. Mari Fairweather. My brother, Robert and I were traveling here from Portland. He is my only family. We had hopes of opening a general store here."

Thunder Heart watched as her eyes got a far away look in them before filling with tears. Her chin quivered as the tears fell. He could see as she clutched the cup tightly between her small, trembling hands that she was fearfully reliving the worst moment of her life.

"Oh, John, it was so horrible," she cried. "The wind was so strong. It tossed the ship to and fro like a toy and drove huge waves over our ship. When our cabin began to flood, the first mate, Mr. Martin took us to the Captain's cabin above deck. We had just entered the cabin when the wind screamed, and as I placed my hands over my ears, the main mast broke and came crashing down onto the cabin. The last thing I saw before I was tossed into the sea was Robert attempting to save the cabin boy as he clung to the broken ship's wheel, being swept over board. Once in the water, I grabbed the nearest floating object I could reach. I believe it was a piece of deck rail. The water was so cold that I pulled myself up onto it. I found some rope, and I wrapped it around myself and hung on with all my might."

"I guess that was what really saved you," Thunder replied. "I had to use my knife to cut you loose. Would you like some more tea, Miss Fairweather?"

Dropping her eyes, she blushed. Again. "You may call me Mari. And yes, I would like some more tea, but may I dress first, kind sir?"

John blushed before sputtering out, "Oh yes, yes. I'll step outside while you dress." As he passed her now washed and dried clothing to her, he looked deeply into her eyes.

As their gazes locked, Mari stated breathlessly, "Thank you, John."

Thunder Heart suddenly felt his world spin. His heart started to pound and heat pooled within his gut. He had never felt this way before, not even with his beloved Dancing Moon. He smiled briefly, grabbed his coat off the hook by the door, and stepped outside. The rain had stopped, but the day remained cloudy and cold. He walked out back to the privy and sat there thinking. He was at least out of the wind, he thought while he did his business. He smiled to himself, thinking that it sure beat going behind a bush up on the mountain. Then he thought about Mari, and how she made him feel such a mixture of conflicting things that he needed to sort out.

She was beautiful, but she was a white woman. He knew how the people in Vancouver would shun her if she stayed too long alone in a cabin with an Indian, even if he were a healer.

By the time he was done with his constitutional, he had made some decisions. He would have to get her into town as soon as possible, but she could not travel that far yet. If she didn't come down with a fever and the weather cleared, maybe they could make the journey the day after tomorrow.

As he walked back to the cabin he decided he would go hunting tomorrow morning. Mari needed meat to regain her strength. Before he entered the cabin he politely rapped on the door.

Mari answered, "Come in."

Opening the door and stepping inside, he paused for a moment as his eyes beheld the frail beauty that was Mari Fairweather. Now wearing her ocean-bleached night dress underneath his flannel shirt, she stood beside the fire, warming her hands. His glance took her in from top to bottom, that is to say, from the top of her head with its silken hair that caressed her small shoulders to her tiny bare feet.

She looked up at him and blushed, again, before stepping aside as he bent to put more wood on the fire for her. "Thank you again, John," she stated, "For rescuing me."

He nodded and restated, "I am a healer, Mari. I could not and would not turn my back on any living thing that needed my help."

She looked at the floor and stated again, "I understand, John. But I do owe you my life, though, and I am truly grateful. May I have some more of that tea now?"

John poured her a cup of tea, and while she sat on the chair at the table sipping it, he hung his coat and started a stew. She studied this handsome hero who had found her, and as he prepared their meal of rabbit and vegetables, she decided she wanted to know more about him.

"So," she began. "Tell me about yourself, where you're from and about your family. I have never met a real Indian before."

John sat cross-legged on the rug before the fire, poking the coals. "Well, I come from a place called Mist Mountain, where I live in a cabin that sits on a treeless plateau that overlooks our village town of Mist Valley. I have three younger brothers and two sisters."

"Is your home very far from here?"

Smiling up at her, he answered, "Yes Mari, far to the east of here, and to tell you just how far, I will say this: It took me almost a month of hard riding to get here."

"And what about your family?"

"My father is a holy man, like a minister, and the Peace Chief of our village, and my mother is a healer. My Uncle Red Fox is our tribal chief, but since he is away a lot of the time working with the loggers, my father often handles his duties as well."

Finishing her tea and handing the cup back to him, she wondered, "Did you ever go to school?" She was genuinely curious, because John seemed so intelligent, and she didn't think Indians even went to school.

"Yes, I have been schooled by a black robe priest and by both my parents, and by my two uncles."

"They must have been some really good teachers, because you speak so well, John."

"Thank you, Mari. I actually..." He paused, shaking his head. "I don't want you to think I am bragging."

"It's okay, John. I really want to know."

Thunder looked deep into Mari's eyes. Her whole body was entirely sunrise red by this point. Finding no malice in her, he continued. "I speak several languages: Cheyenne, Sioux, English, Latin and some French as well as some other regional tribal languages."

"Wow, John. I can hardly even read myself. My family didn't think a girl needed a formal education. My brother... he was the one. He had a great head for figures and read a lot." Her eyes filling again with tears, she stated, "He used to read to me as I cleaned the store."

John reached out and patted her hand. "Mari, don't. Don't start thinking that all is lost quite yet. If you survived that storm, maybe he did too. The wind tossed the sea around a lot that night. He could have even landed on the other side of the bay."

"Do you really think so?!" she gasped as she wiped the tears from her cheeks.

"It's a good chance, Mari. When you are stronger, we'll go into town and check for him there."

"How will we get there? Do you have a horse, John?"

"Oh, yes. I have a fine one. He's stabled behind the house. After dinner, you can help me check on him if you feel up to it, but only for a short time, okay?"

"That would be wonderful, John. I do love horses." Readjusting her position to get closer to the fire to cover her feet, she decided to see if Thunder would tell her more about himself. So she pried, smiling, "John, tell me what brought you here to this side of the mountains."

Thunder Heart didn't know just how much he should tell her, but seeing that she was genuinely interested, he began, "Well, two weeks ago I started having dreams of a powerful storm and my father felt that it was my destiny to come here, and once here, my path would be made known to me. When I got into town, my friend Sergeant O'Malley gave me directions and the key to his cabin and here I am."

"Was there anything else you saw in your dream?"

"Well, there was something else, Mari. The night before the storm hit, I dreamed of you."

Mari's eyes jerked up to his and a tremor took her, shaking her all over. John jumped up and grabbed a blanket, wrapping it around her before pulling her closer to the fire. Once he had her settled he took some fruit out of his war bag and handed it to her. Then he retrieved a book from off the shelf above the bed and sat down beside her. He could see she still trembled, so he drew her against his side, rubbing his hand up and down her arm. "Hey, how about I read to you while you eat?"

She smiled weakly and relaxed into him. "Okay, John. That would be nice."

She was in shock at his admission, yet she found she was comforted by his presence. Did he really dream of her, she wondered? Could he have been sent here just to help her? Did God really answer prayers that way? She pondered all these things as she nibbled on a mixture of dried fruit and pine nuts.

Snuggled close to John's side, Mari stared at the flickering fire while Thunder read the beginnings of *Moby Dick* to her. She relaxed, listening to his wonderfully rich, deep voice, but she couldn't concentrate on the story. Her mind was on her brother. She knew John was trying his best to help her relax and heal, but she was so worried that her brother had died. Her last memory of Robert was of him reaching out towards the cabin boy as they were swept overboard. She prayed silently that if he were alive, that he hadn't lost hope of finding her.

Suddenly, John stopped reading and reached over to the fire to stir the stew and add a few potatoes he had gathered earlier from the root cellar. He also poured her another cup of tea and handed it to her before sitting back down to continue reading.

The wind had picked up once more and it started raining again. It would be a long day, she thought, and yet she found John's company soothing. She had met her share of overly-flirtatious men and drunks while living in a mining town outside of Seattle, to not know a nice one when she met him. Yet then again, he was an Indian, and didn't they rape, kill, and scalp people? They didn't read and speak different languages. But he looked like an Indian. Long, black hair, deep dark... wait a minute, blue eyes?

Suddenly, she blurted out, "John, why do you have blue eyes?"

Taken off guard by her question, he looked at her puzzled for a moment then thoughtfully replied: "Well, it's probably because my mother's father was a white man and he had blue eyes, I was told."

She looked at him with bright, questioning eyes, and he began to relate to her the story of his grandparents. As he told her story after story about his family and the love stories connected to them, she began to feel a part of it all, and wished she could make a journey there someday and meet the people of Mist Valley.

After talking for what seemed like hours, Thunder Heart asked her if she felt like talking about her life and family.

Mari couldn't understand why she felt so comfortable with John, but she did, so she took a deep breath and started in. She told him of how her father had sold his family farm in Kansas and moved west to the gold fields, how he had met her mother. After he found enough gold, they were married and started their general store.

She related how as a family they had turned the store into a profitable business, but then the influenza hit and they lost both their parents and a baby sister. They tried to work the store alone, but there were too many memories there. So, hearing of the gold strikes up north they sold out and set off to start a new life.

Mari started to shiver again, and John reached up to feel her forehead. "You, my sweet miss, have a fever. I want you to eat and then I will make you a strong tea to bring it down. Please turn your back to me."

She looked at him, puzzled, but complied. He leaned over, and laying his ear to her back, asked her to take a deep breath. She complied, but it brought about a spell of coughing.

"Your lungs are congested," he stated with concern. "I'll give you something to help you breathe better, as well as bring your fever down. It'll taste bad though, so I'll sweeten it with a lot of honey. The honey will also help you heal."

"I didn't know honey had healing properties," she stated,, her brow furrowed in serious thought.

Thunder couldn't resist the opportunity to tease her, and stated with a very serious face. "Oh yes, Mari. Have you ever seen a sick bee?"

"No. Oh. Oh, you silly goose you. You're pulling my leg." she playfully swatted at him while falling over in a fit of giggles.

Thunder was filled with longing at the beautiful sound that came from this lovely maiden. While a smile spread across his lips, he began to grow quiet. He was not sure he could trust the feelings that she brought back to life within him. It had been a very long time since he had a woman, and he so wanted to kiss her full, pink lips.

After they had eaten, and she'd taken her medicinal tea, he wrapped her in a blanket, put his spare moccasins on her feet, and escorted her to the privy. On the way back, they stopped briefly to give the horse some oats.

The stallion was glad to see his master, bobbing his head and swishing his tail happily. Mari reached up and scratched him behind the ears, and the powerful animal nuzzled her lovingly. Smiling, Thunder watched Mari with the horse, thinking that she was such a gentle soul, but when he observed her shivering again, he swung her up into his arms and carried her back into the house.

Once again in the cabin, they reclined before the warm fire. Mari loved the feel of the bear skin rug on her legs as she rested upon it. Snug beneath a soft trade blanket of red and black stripes, she listened attentively as Thunder again read to her.

Sitting with his back up against the wall, Thunder was overcome by fatigue and drifted off to sleep, allowing the book to slip almost soundlessly to the floor.

It was during this time that Mari continued to study her savior. He was so very handsome, broad-shouldered, and tall with well-defined muscles. He made her heart race and her stomach flutter. She loved his deep voice and his soft touch and gentle ways. He was so kind and attentive. She wondered again if he was really sent by God to find her. She found herself wishing she could stay with him forever, but she knew how white people treated Indians, and she feared they would harm him for helping or even being with her. But she couldn't keep from gazing at his handsome face, and wished she could kiss his full, sensuous lips. She took a chance. While leaning over him, being careful not to wake him, she brushed his lips with hers ever-so-lightly. However, to her shock, he felt her touch upon his lips. This caused him to reach out with his strong arms and pull her to him, deepening the kiss. Blushing deeply, she pushed against his chest, breaking the kiss. Awestruck by her first ever kiss, she placed her fingers to her lips.

Turning her face away from him, she said, "Oh my, oh my. I should never have done that. I don't know what got into me, John. I have never done anything like that before. Please, forgive me. You must think me brazen, and flippantly forward."

John took a deep breath and released it slowly. He didn't want her to see how much she affected him. Yet she did affect him; greatly. Smiling, he reached over and stroked her hair, and didn't stop until he felt her relax. Then, speaking low and soft, he said, "Mari I was meant to find you. Don't be embarrassed. You just did what I'd wanted to do ever since I found you on the beach. You are the loveliest woman I have ever met. You don't hold any hatred in your heart for my people, and I could lose myself in those big sky blue pools you call eyes."

Turning back to him, she looked once again into his intense gaze, and that was his undoing. He gently pulled her over onto his lap and began kissing her with so much passion that it took her breath away. Breathless and shivering, Mari clung to his strong, warm body. Soon, relaxed and warm, they both fell asleep by the fire.

Later that night, she awakened, and by the flickering firelight, she studied her handsome hero some more as she absently rubbed her finger over her lips, remembering the feel of his kisses. His face was ruggedly chiseled, with high cheek bones, a firm square jaw, and sensual, full lips. She remembered how, when he looked at her with those deep blue eyes of his, they took her breath away, as if he could see into her very soul. His shoulders were wide and his arms well-muscled, but it was his hands that made her shudder with excitement. They were large and strong, with the strength to cause great harm, but he touched her only with tenderness. His stomach was flat and corded with muscle and his thighs were large and rock-hard from walking over long distances. She smiled to herself as she considered belonging to such a man as him. She had hoped when she came to this new land that she would find a fine husband, but if her brother was dead, she had no way of making a living and no family to take her in. If John did not want her, she supposed she would have to find employment, but the thought of working in a saloon made her shudder. She was still a maiden, and had wanted to save herself for true love.

She snuggled closer to John, who upon feeling her move, pulled his buffalo robe tighter around her as she again laid her head into his lap.

John held her tenderly, feeling her warmth next to him. She was so desirable, and he longed to bury himself in her sweetness, making her his forever, but he knew how the whites looked upon white women who took up with Indians, and she was far too sweet to suffer such injustice.

But for some reason, the spirits had brought them together, and until the spirits told him differently, he would hold her close and keep her safe from everything and everyone; even if it cost him his very life.

CHAPTER 16: THE WHITE MAN'S WORLD

The next morning was wrapped in golden, warm sunshine, and Thunder decided since Mari felt stronger and her fever was down, they would make the long trek into town, but Mari wanted to spend the day by the sea. She hoped she would find more of her clothes. After having Mari dress in his extra clothes, he placed her on his horse. Then with practiced grace, he mounted up behind her and they were off.

The path down to the bay was not a difficult one, and Thunder Heart found himself deeply enjoying the feel of Mari's body as she rode in front of him. It was the sweetest of tortures. They rode along the beach until the sun was high in the sky, but saw no signs of useful wreckage or beached bodies. Mari was so pleased by this that she asked Thunder to help her down so she could tend to nature and then walk the water's edge. With her duties attended to, she ran for the water's edge, her bare feet dancing in the waves as they lapped the sand. Thunder enjoyed watching her as she laughed and danced with little hopping steps as the cold water met her toes.

"John, come dance with me!" she squealed as another wave of icy water covered her toes.

"Mari, you mustn't get too chilled. Come now, we must leave before the sun goes down."

"No, John. I'm not leaving until you dance with me, right here, right now on this beach. I wish to celebrate life and all that it holds."

Thunder chuckled as he took off his moccasins and went to her, taking her small hands in his. He twirled her around and around, just to hear her giggles, until she stumbled and he caught her in his arms. Unable and unwilling to resist any longer, he cupped her face in his hands and kissed her with all the passion he possessed and she melted within his arms. She was his for the taking, but he could not and would not. His love could only bring her pain. He carried her to the horse and they rode back to the cabin.

That evening, they ate the last of their rabbit stew and sat by the fire, telling each other stories of their childhood. Mari showed him a beautiful abalone shell she had found on the beach, and he promised he would make her a necklace out of it for her. She held it in her hand as she fell asleep in the bed that night. She had not made a fuss when Thunder said she should sleep away from him because passion's temptation was too great for them both, and everything hinged on her finding her brother.

The next day, they rose early, packed up their meager supplies, and rode off for town. Mari thought she looked a sight wearing Thunder's buck skin pants and a red and white checked shirt that was six sizes too big, but Thunder thought he had never seen a more beautiful woman in his life. After a short while the wind kept blowing her long hair into his face, so he pulled off a fringe from the buck skins she wore and used it to tie back her hair. She gave him a questioning look, and he replied, "Well, it kept tickling my nose and making my eyes water. I couldn't see where we were going."

"Well," she piped up. "I could ride behind you."

Thunder tightened his hold around her waist and whispered into her ear, "Oh no you don't. I like you right where you are."

Mari giggled and swatted him on the thigh and they rode on.

Though Thunder intended to set a quick pace, he found her wide-eyed wonder of nature refreshing, and so he slowed his pace often, even stopping to point out an animal or a beautiful flower for her enjoyment. They even dismounted a few times and walked awhile because he knew she was unaccustomed to riding for long periods.

Though he had planned to arrive in town before dark, he now thought better of it. After dark would be better for Mari's protection. He would get rooms at a hotel, and there would be fewer tongues to wag about them arriving together. As he held her slender body to him, she leaned her head back against his chest and began to doze.

Placing a kiss on her head, he again pledged to protect her with his life.

The ride to Vancouver took hours, but Mari proved to be far stronger than he had imagined, and they made it into town right at sundown. He took her to the same hotel that he knew had given Indians a room before. After securing adjacent rooms, he ordered her a bath and some supper to be sent up. Once he had her settled, he left to go to the general store to purchase them some new clothes.

When he returned, he knocked on her door, and when she didn't answer, he presumed she had fallen asleep. Taking out the key to her room, he entered quietly to place his packages for her on the table, but when he heard a soft noise coming from behind him he turned and was met by a dazzling smile, shimmering auburn tresses, big blue eyes, and enticing curves all wrapped up in a calico sheet.

Oh, Ma'heo'o, he thought. She was so stunning. She took his breath away, and he wanted her with every fiber of his being.

Stammering as he felt his blood heat and pool deep in his groin he stated, "I, I bought you some things. I hope they fit. I was thinking that if you would like, and feel up to it, we could go to the hospital tomorrow and look for your brother."

Suddenly feeling melancholy and guilty over her lustful thoughts toward this wonderful man who treated her with such tenderness, she dropped her gaze and tucked the sheet more securely around her slender form before reaching for the packages with trembling fingers.

"Oh, thank you, John for everything you have done for me, but these things must have cost you a fortune."

"It was not that much, really. Hurry, now. We need to eat and then retire. Tomorrow morning I'll meet you in the dinning room down stairs for breakfast, okay?"

"Yes, John. That sounds wonderful. I'll meet you there at seven. Now shoo, so I can change." She giggled.

As he left the room, Mari quickly opened the packages. At awe at his generosity, she took the night gown and lavender wrapper he had chosen for her, and stepped behind the dressing screen. She flung the sheet over the screen and pulled the silk gown over her head. It slid down easily over her small frame and she thought she had never felt anything so heavenly sinful in her life. After running her hands down over her curves she rapidly put on the matching lavender satin robe.

Thunder returned quickly, carrying the food tray through the door that joined their rooms, and noticed the pretty sheet flung over the top of the black lacquered Chinese dressing screen that stood in the corner of her room. His mind instantly remembered the feel of her naked body next to his. It was a good thing he had set the tray down, because when she came out from behind the screen he was stunned by her radiance. Seeing her dressed in the flowing nightgown and satin wrapper he had bought for her, and her hair brushed and hanging loosely around her slender shoulders, he wanted to forget about the food and take her into his arms right then. Instead, he drew on all of his training as a warrior and reminded himself firmly that she was a maiden. After taking some well-needed deep breaths, he just sat down the tray on the table and quickly took a seat to hide his erection.

Then he stated softly, "Mari, you are so beautiful. Here." He pointed to the chair opposite him. "Come, sit, and eat before it gets cold. "

Feeling a lump grow in her throat just then, all she could say as she blushed prettily was, "Thank you."

That evening, as they ate their supper together, they planned out where they would begin searching for her brother.

When the meal was over, John excused himself from her company, and Mari retired to bed exhausted from the long day. Later that night Mari awakened, gasping for breath. Unable to calm herself enough to fall asleep again, she called out for John. He entered her room quickly and upon seeing her distress, he took her into his arms and sat with her on the bed. Taking up the book he had brought with them from the cabin, he again read to her. Her fever had spiked again, and John was glad he had obtained adjoining rooms so he could keep an eye on her condition. Once she had fallen back to sleep, he went back to his own room.

Weary, but still unable to relax, he opened his door and called for the hired boy, who was sitting in the hallway dozing, to bring him up a warm bath. The boy of mixed background was poorly and thin, yet he brought the heavy buckets up the stairs without complaint, and was so delighted when Thunder Heart tipped him a whole dollar that he could not help but bubble forth with questions.

"Is that perdy lady your wife, mister? Is she sick or some'pin?" He blushed deeply, much in the way of Mari, to have asked such personal questions.

John, flashing the youth a broad smile, whispered, "No, she is not my wife, but I sure am hoping. She is very sick, though, and I am taking her to see a doctor tomorrow. Please don't say anything, okay? I don't want people to talk." The boy nodded his understanding and left by the back stairs.

John poured the water into the old wooden tub that sat behind his dressing screen. He then stripped off his soft buck skin pants and sank into the hot water. Letting out a deep sigh, he thought, oh *Ma'heo'o*, this feels so good. No wonder women love tub baths so much. Once done, he snuggled beneath the covers on the soft feather bed, and was just about to fall asleep when he heard Mari cry out again. "Nooooooo!"

He jumped up and flew to her bedside again. She was kneeling in the middle of the bed clutching the bed clothes to her chest. Her eyes were wild with fear and she flew into his arms when he came close and spoke her name. He felt her trembling beneath his hands as he held her close. While he stroked her hair he whispered soft loving words to her in Cheyenne. Taking a deep breath he tried to leave but she continued to cling to him, crying.

"Please, please don't leave me, John," she sobbed as she clung to the security of his strong arms. "I felt like I was drowning in the darkness again."

With a wistful smile, John relaxed back onto the bed again, pulling her close to his side. Oh, how good she felt there, he thought. It was like she had been made just for him. He wondered if the spirits had indeed done just that. He knew he should not get too attached to her, but he was fast losing his heart. His body was already lost, and he fought to control its response to her. It was a good thing that he was wearing a night shirt for once, because she didn't get comfortable again until her head was lying in his lap. As her trembling stopped, Mari drifted off to sleep once again and John returned to his room, but it was far into the night before he surrendered to his dreams.

CHAPTER 17: MARI'S BROTHER

The next morning, Thunder met Mari downstairs for breakfast. She could hardly believe her eyes. He was dressed as a white man— in a pair black whip cord pants that hugged his large, firm thighs seductively, and a white flannel shirt that was stretched tightly across his broad shoulders. A smile crossed her lips when she noticed he still wore his moccasins. His hair was pulled back and tied at the nape of his neck, its length hidden under his shirt. Smiling broadly, her eyes never leaving his, she glided over to stand before him. He beamed back at her with a twinkle in his eyes as he assessed her up and down. She was wearing the yellow cotton dress he had bought her. Its square neckline accented with tiny white lace drew attention to, but didn't reveal any of her cleavage. At her tiny waist, she had pinned a white daisy from her room, and her hair was tied back loosely with a bright yellow matching ribbon she had found in the box with her dress.

"I see you are feeling better this morning, Mari," he stated with barely-contained longing in his voice.

Their eyes locked briefly and Mari knew that he felt she was beautiful.

"Yes, I do. Thank you for being with me last night, John. I do hope those horrible nightmares go away soon. I can hardly bare them. Oh, and by the way... you look very nice yourself, this morning." She held her hand out to him.

Taking it, he led her to a table in the back, on the far left side of the dining room by a window. She lowered her eyes as Thunder Heart helped her to sit. She could feel his breath next to her temple as he whispered in her ear, "Oh, sweet one, you look like sunshine in that dress."

Mari blushed and let out a tiny giggle that Thunder thought sounded like the tinkling of tiny silver bells.

They ordered and ate silently, occasionally flashing looks and smiles at each other. He knew she was hopeful that she would find her brother, but deep within him, he had a nagging sense of dread.

When they were finished, they walked to the livery down the street where John hired a buggy to take them to the hospital. The ride was pleasant, but upon reaching the hospital, they were both overwhelmed by the number of tents erected on the grounds.

"Oh, John," she gasped, taking hold of his arm to steady herself. "There are so many hurt people here. How will we ever find my brother?"

"We will ask, and if need be, we will search every tent and room. Come on. We won't find him standing here." He took off at a determined pace.

Mari followed along behind Thunder as he flagged down a rapidly moving nurse. "Madam, where can we find the head doctor?" he asked her.

She pointed to a tent that had a red cross painted on it. "He's there," she guided.

"Thank you miss!" he called out to her as she ran off to attend to her duties. Thunder took Mari's hand in support, and they walked toward the tent, and he was so glad he had, because the closer they got to the tent, the more she shook. Just outside the tent, he wrapped an arm about her shoulders and hugged her gently stating, "It will all be okay. I am here, Small One".

She took a shuddering breath and tried to compose herself but she could not let go of his hand.

Once inside, they found a very haggard-looking elderly gentleman sitting at a desk covered with medical charts.

"Excuse us, sir, Thunder said. "We are here to inquire about a man who was aboard a ship that wrecked in the storm?"

Dr. Wills lifted his tired eyes to them, and upon seeing Mari, he rose from his seat and offered it to her.

"Here, young lady, come and sit. I am Dr. Wills, chief physician here at St. Mary's. How can I help you?"

Mari took a trembling breath and told the doctor her tale from where she and her brother were swept from the ship into the rolling sea until she was rescued by John Thunder Heart.

"So, there it is, doctor," she said. "If it weren't for John here, I would have perished also. Have you any word of my brother Robert Fairweather or has anyone asked about me?"

The doctor took a deep, weary breath and shook his head.

"My dear, there has been no inquiries for you by anyone. As to your brother, I don't remember coming across his name. However, there are three places in which to look. The list of patients at the main desk of the hospital, the tents marked with a blue stripe containing the severely injured, and the big tent down by the trees where the unclaimed bodies are."

Mari blanched, and her chin started to quiver. The doctor observed John as he comforted her and assessed her for a return of her fever.

"John," asked Dr. Wills. "I have noticed how you just now assessed your charge. Are you a medicine man?"

Thunder Heart straightened his spine and looked the doctor squarely in the eyes before he replied, "Dr. Wills, I am a healer like yourself. I have been very well educated, sir, however there are still some things I wish to learn. I have noted that you are very short-staffed here and there are a number of people and Indians that still need help. May I extend my hand in aid to you and them, sir?"

Mari quickly chimed in, "Oh, Doctor, John is very learned. He speaks English, Sioux, Cheyenne, Latin, French, and some other Indian languages. He also reads and writes very well too."

"Well, if that don't beat all." Dr. Wills shook his head and stroked his graying beard. "You know John, I could use your help at that. And what about you, my dear? Have you a place to stay, or family here in the area?"

"No, sir," Mari stated. "I have no one, save for my brother. John has been most generous to have obtained a room for me at a small hotel, but I don't know how long I can stay without any finances."

"Mari," John patiently explained. "The room at Ms. Nelly's boarding house is paid up well in advance and you owe me nothing. Later after we are done looking for your brother, we can go by the bank. Surely your brother did not carry all his finances in cash, and if he was truly the great businessman you told me of, he would have had a line of credit sent by wire to the bank."

"Yes my dear," extolled Dr. Wills. "That is indeed sound advice. You should do just that. And you, young man… report back here to me when you can and I will put you to work straight away."

Thunder Heart stretched out his hand and the good doctor shook it soundly. Thunder knew instantly that the good doctor was an honorable man by the way he acted towards them, a man he could respect and trust. Smiling gratefully, he replied, "Thank you, sir. I will pick up my medical bag from the hotel and return as quickly as I can."

With that, Thunder and Mari left to search for Robert. They checked everywhere except the tent of the dead, but he was nowhere to be found. So, with much trepidation, they finally went to search among the dead. Thunder Heart did the lifting of the sheets, only letting Mari see anyone who fit her brother's description. Suddenly, as they were about to end their search, Mari let out a scream and clasped to the floor by the body of her beloved brother. The ship's first mate Martin also lay nearby, along with the cabin boy Robert attempted to rescue. The ship's captain was never found.

CHAPTER 18: NELLY

The shock of seeing her dead brother had caused Mari to faint dead away. Thunder Heart swept her up into his arms and carried her outside to the awaiting carriage. Once outside in the fresh air, she came to, but she clung to him like a child, weeping so hard that his shirt became soaked with her tears. He, with some difficulty, got them both into the buggy and drove quickly back to the hotel. When they arrived at the hotel, he gave the now familiar errand boy another dollar and commanded him to take the buggy back to the livery. The boy quickly complied, as Thunder carried Mari upstairs to her room. He gently laid her in the middle of her bed, took off her shoes and covered her with a warm blanket.

As he turned to leave, she grabbed hold of his hand and begged him saying, "PLEASE, please John, don't leave me. I can't bear being alone right now."

Patting her hand, he told her, "Sweet one. I do not intend to leave you for long. I only wish to go to the kitchen for some hot water for tea. I will hurry and be right back." Hovering above her small, trembling form, Thunder's heart ached for her. He brushed the stray strands of her silken hair from her forehead and placed a chaste kiss there before saying, "Rest Mari, please."

With that, she released him, pulled a pillow into her arms, and rolled into a small ball and wept anew.

Thunder, shaking his head, took a deep, cleansing breath before he rushed out of the room and down the back stairs to the kitchen where he found the hotel owner's wife preparing dinner.

She was an elderly, rotund woman who wore her graying hair in a tight bun at the back of her neck and a white apron tied around her waist. Thunder, not wanting to bother the very busy woman covered in flour, finally cleared his throat and said, "Excuse me madam. May I have a tea kettle of boiling water?"

The plump woman looked up from her work at the stove and ran her sharp appraising eyes over him before answering, "Yur that fella who brung the lady here yesterday, aren't ya?"

"Yes, madam," Thunder said. "I'm John Thunder Heart. I took the lady, Mari, to the hospital today to see if her brother had survived the shipwreck also, but she found him among the dead. I want to brew her some herbal tea to help her rest while I go and make arrangements for his burial."

"Oh, the poor wee dear," she stated as she took a hot pad from the side board and retrieved the kettle. Taking it with her to the cupboard that sat near the stove, she obtained a medium-sized teapot and poured it full of hot water.

"This be enough fer ya, son?" she asked as she handed the pot to him along with a cup.

"Yes, Madam, and thank you."

"You're very welcome, Mr. Heart. If you have a need for any thin else just tell the staff that Ms. Nelly says it's okay."

"Thanks again Madam. I am very pleased to make your acquaintance."

As he turned to go, she piped up, "Ya know, son, its kinda queer ta have an Indian take such an interest in a white lady. Not that it's bad or nothin'. It's just we be runnin' a proper house and all."

John stiffened. "Madam I am a healer, and just because I found the lady half-dead and cared for her does not make my relationship with her improper. And yes, Ms. Nelly, I am a Cheyenne, and being such, among my people it's a great wrong to withhold aid where it is needed. And personally as a healer, I am honor-bound to give aid and comfort to any wounded thing, and she, my good woman, has been grievously wounded."

The elderly woman blushed and dropped her head. "I'm truly sorry, son. I had to ask ye, ya see. I'm right sorry about her brother, though. Now, will ye both be stayin' on here a spell?"

"Yes, madam, I must provide aid for her until she has her affairs in order. As for me, well, I will be assisting Dr. Wills at the hospital with the many wounded and sick until this crisis is over."

The elderly lady reached out and patted his arm and smiled sweetly. Her keen, green eyes aglow. "Ye are a rare bird, John Thunder Heart. Rare indeed. Ye and the lass are welcome to stay here as long as ye like. My Jim'll ward off them tongue-waggers."

John, smiling down at her, patted her shoulder softly, then stated, "Thank you very much, Ms. Nelly."

"Call me Nelly from now on. Now off with ya. I gots a meal to prepare. When it's done I'll be sendin' little Billy Blue Hawk up with a tray and a bucket of warm water for the lady."

"Thanks, Nelly, for everything. That would be wonderful, thank you."

Thunder trotted up the back stairs and into the room. Setting down the tea pot and cup on the small table by the window, he rifled through his pack on the floor until he found the right herbs that would help Mari. He was never without his bag of medicines, and even though it was well stocked, he knew if he were to properly aid the good doctor, he would need to go into the forest to gather more, and soon. Some herbs, however, needed to be dried or prepared in a special way to be of any use to the sick. He made a mental note to ask if anyone new of an herbalist in the area.

After sprinkling a large amount of ground chamomile, Valerian root, and sassafras root into the teapot, he added some honey from the honey pot on the table and set the teapot aside for a while to steep. He walked quietly into Mari's room and found her just as he had left her. She looked so small and heartbroken, like a wounded bird, and as he gazed down upon her, he was filled with a rush of protectiveness, and yes, even love for her. She had no one now, and for the first time since he had found her, he knew he felt more for her than just being bound by honor to care for her. He wanted to keep her with him always. He loved her. He went and sat down on the bed beside her.

Upon feeling the bed move, Mari rolled over and laid her head in his lap again. He wiped away her tears with his thumb and tenderly caressed her cheek with the back of his fingers. Then leaning over, he brushed his lips softly across hers before placing a kiss on the top of her head.

He meant it to be very brotherly, but when Mari gazed up at him with those big, innocent blue eyes of hers so full of tears and pain, he was undone. Cradling her small face between his hands, he brushed her lips with his again. Filled with need and a sudden desire she didn't understand, she reached up and took hold of his face pulling him closer to her and deepened the kiss. He pulled her into his arms then and kissed her with all the passion within him.

Suddenly, she broke the kiss, breathless. "Oh, John I love you so. Stay with me, hold me, show me your love. No man has ever kissed me like that before." Blushing deeply at her brazen outburst, she dropped her eyes from his gaze and stated in a low whisper, "Truthfully, John. No man has ever kissed me before."

Holding her securely within his arms he silently rocked her gently for quite a while, running his hand up and down her back before he uttered softly into her long silky hair, "Oh, Mari, I care for you also. But you are a maiden and I will not take from you that which should be saved for marriage."

"John, are you asking me to marry you?"

"I would be most honored to have you for my wife, Mari. But we do not know each other very well yet, and I don't want to make you my woman only to have your feelings change once all the pain has left your life."

"John, my feelings for you will not change. I fell in love with you the first moment I saw you standing before the fire in the Mounties' cabin, and when I looked into your eyes so full of gentleness and caring, well, I knew my heart was lost. Somehow, deep inside, I knew you were sent to find me."

Sweeping a stay hair from her face, he kissed her again, softly, but completely. "Mari," he whispered huskily into her ear. "I have some tea for you to drink and food will be sent up to us soon. I want you to drink all the tea, eat something, and then rest, okay? And while you are resting, I'll go and make arrangements for your brother."

She sighed deeply and nodded her head. "I don't feel much like eating right now, John, but the tea sounds good." John got up and quickly brought her a cup of steaming tea. She reached out to take the cup, and she observed a strange, pinched look on Thunder's face and asked, "What is it? What's wrong?"

"Well, I wish this tea was more palatable," he said. "Its a very strong medicine to help you sleep, and not one that tastes or smells very good, I'm afraid."

Mari smiled as she took the floral china cup from his large hand and said, "John, your teas never taste good, but they sure do help. Thank you." She sat in bed, sipping her tea and feeling its warmth flow through her body as John sat in the chair beside her bed, reading to her as he had done so in the cabin. They were about halfway through their book about the white whale when Mari began to relax and become sleepy. As John saw her start to doze, he took the empty cup from her and sat it on the bedside table. Tucking the covers around her, he placed a gentle kiss upon her cheek, then he picked up his medical bag and left the room to attend to the sad, but necessary business of making funeral arrangements.

CHAPTER 19: DR. JOHN

Walking determinedly down the street toward the livery, Thunder Heart again met the helpful youth. The boy was such a poor-looking waif with his torn knickers, dirty home-spun shirt and faded cap that sat cock-eyed upon his thick, shaggy mop of dark hair. Yet Thunder's heart always seemed to melt when he saw him. He guessed it was the fact that as hard as the boy's life was, he always had a smile on his face.

As the boy fell into step beside him, he piped up saying, "Hi, sir. Is the lady feelin' better? I'm rightly sorry, sir, to hear about her losing her brother."

John stopped, and smiling down at the lad, reached out a hand to him. The boy took it and gave it a firm shake. "Thank you son," John said. "She is some better but it will take time for her to get over her many losses. My name is John Thunder Heart. And yours is?"

"Oh, oh ooh," the boy mouthed, his eyes widening with sudden understanding. John was an Indian too. "My name is Billy, aw, Billy Blue Hawk, sir, and I'm right glad to meet you. And thanks again for payin' me so good, sir, but I had a real hard time convincing my ma how it was I got it."

Smiling, John said, "Well Billy, my pa says that anyone who works hard should be rewarded well."

"Well, Mister, I'm sure glad for the pay. It's been hard on my ma since my Pa left. Ma works for Ms. Nelly too, but no one knows she's my ma. Her bein' a white woman an all. Ms. Nelly says she needs to find another man and can't do that if folks knew she was married before to an Indian. Ms. Nelly sure is kind to me though. She don't treat Indians like dirt like some folks do around here."

"Do you go to school, Billy?"

"No, sir, they wouldn't 'cept me, so ma teaches me when she has time. I can read and write and cipher well enough, but I wish I could learn some more so I could get me a real job someday."

"What do you want to do for a living, Billy?"

"I wants to be a newspaper man, findin' and reportin' the news. Maybe even work for the Vancouver post someday."

John noticed the boy's steps slowing as they walked and observed his downcast face. "What's wrong, Billy?"

"It's just..." he said, looking down at the dust covering his worn shoes. "It's all a dream. Ma says I gots ta keep my head outta the clouds."

John squatted down and looked the boy right in the eyes.

"Look here, son, dreams are good to have. They keep us striving to become more than we are. Once, I wanted to be the best bowman in my tribe. So I practiced really hard, so hard, in fact, that my fingers bled, but finally I learned to shoot 5 arrows faster than some men can pull and fire a gun."

"Wow, Mister," the boy gasped with huge eyes.

John, laying his hand on Billy's shoulder, stated, "Billy, as we grow, our dreams shape us, and they change as we change and grow up. Now, even though my people would call me a great warrior or hunter for my skill with a bow, it is my love of healing and learning that defines me as a man, and I find my honor in doing that. Dreams are good things to have Billy, even for mothers."

"Wow, thanks mister. Is there anythin' I can do for ya today?"

Rising, John said, "Well, yes, Billy, there is. Can you point me to the nearest undertaker? I need to make arrangements for Miss Mari's brothers burial."

"Oh sure, I can do that," Billy stated. "That's old Mr. Jenkins. He has a place just down from the livery over there." The boy pointed to a gray building about half a block away. "Well I gots to be going, Mister. Can we talk again later? I want my ma to meet ya."

"Yes, Billy, we will talk again."

Billy ran back to the boarding house and John walked on to the undertaker's place down the street.

John Thunder Heart truly realized he had grown up in a wonderful place. He had been loved and encouraged in everything, and though he was not well thought of in the white man's world, he had yet to endure the prejudice that young Billy had.

It didn't take long to make the arrangements with the tall, sallow-faced undertaker, and soon he was returning to the livery to retrieve his horse for the ride out to the hospital to claim the body. Once there, he met briefly with Dr. Wills, and made introductory contact with the other staff.

Dr. Wills hadn't really thought Thunder would return, but he wasn't sad that he did. He truly did need the help. Smiling, he tossed Thunder a white lab coat and said, "Put this on, son, and let's go see to the Indian tent. I haven't been able to do much with them, I'm afraid. I can't speak their languages. Did you bring your bag with you?"

"Why, yes, sir. It's on my horse. I'll go and retrieve it and be right back."

When he returned they walked across the tent crowded lawn to a large tent on the far side of the grounds next to the forest.

Once there, John was appalled by the condition of the tent and of the patients that lay upon the bare cots. There were twenty people crammed into the tent around a portable Ben Franklin that sat in the center. Next to it, there was a small table upon which sat a chipped porcelain pitcher and wash pan. John saw immediately what needed to be done. Not paying any mind to Dr. Wills, he headed right back outside and grabbed the nearest nurse.

"Miss, have someone bring a kettle of water and twenty tin cups along with firewood and blankets to this tent right away!"

The young nurse blanched. "Sir, we don't have cups to spare, nor blankets neither, but I will send you wood and water."

John nodded politely and said, "Thank you, miss." Then he went back into the tent where he quickly took charge. First he asked who could speak English. Hands rose. Then he asked who could speak Cheyenne or Suquamish. Many raised their hands. "Good," he spoke in English, then Cheyenne. Taking note of all the hands, he nodded his approval to each one.

"I am Thunder Heart of the northern Cheyenne, son of the Mist Woman who lives on the other side of the mountains. I, like her, am a healer, and singer of my people, and I have come to help you."

Dr. Wills watched as John got everyone's complete attention and confidence. First, John took a wooded bowl from one patient and filled it with burning herbs. Then he took a feather from another patient's hair and used it to direct the smoke from the burning herbs toward each patient, essentially bathing each patient with the smoke as he chanted softly in a soothing melody.

Dr. Wills was just about to interrupt, when John set the bowl down on the stove and went over to an elderly woman. There he laid his hand upon her head, and while feeling for fever, he asked her where her injuries were, but she was too weak to speak. He removed her thin cover and ran his hands over her body. Noting her wince in pain as he touched her right arm, he assessed it further and found that her arm and collar bone were broken. While he did this, she started coughing, and John didn't like the sound of the way it rattled deep in her chest.

Frowning with concern, he turned to Dr. Wills and asked, "Will you aid me in setting her arm, Doctor? I must pull it straight without moving the shoulder. Her collar bone is also broken. Once that is done I will attend to her consumption."

"Very impressive son," Dr. Wills remarked, "But why did you use the smoke and chants?" He aided with the woman's arm.

"You see, doctor, we, the Indian people, believe that when a person is ill it affects the whole being. The smoke is from burning sweet grass and sage which purifies the air. The chants are prayers that set the person's spirit at ease and call for divine aid for the patient as well as the healer. As you know, doctor, God is the true healer. We are just his eyes, ears, and hands."

In no time, they had set and wrapped the woman's arm, and John brewed up a pain-relieving and fever-reducing tea for all the patients with the large kettle of water that the orderly had brought them.

After that, John and Dr. Wills went from patient to patient, setting bones, stitching up cuts and dressing wounds. During all of this, Dr. Wills asked about every treatment and medicinal herb John used.

However, when John came to where a pregnant woman lay burning with fever, he dropped to his knees beside her and began talking in Latin. Dr. Wills, shocked speechless, came to stand over the girl where he watched and listened as John assessed her.

"Doctor," Thunder said in Latin, "This woman's baby is dead. If she is not delivered now, she will die. I am a poor surgeon, sir, but it is my belief that she will not survive a lengthy labor even if I gave her the right herbs to bring about delivery. The babe must be cut out. Doctor, do you have such skill?"

"You mean can I do a caesarian section?"

Thunder Heart nodded in the affirmative.

"Why, yes, John, I do. But have you done such a surgery before?"

"Yes, doctor. I have, but not alone. My mother assisted me."

"And what was the outcome, John?"

"The mother and child recovered fully and she delivered a healthy baby the next year despite my mother's insistence that she not get pregnant again so soon."

"Well, now that could hardly be helped, now could it, young man?"

John turned a serious face up to the doctor. "There are ways to prevent conception, doctor. Women know these things. But she would not take the herbs or precautions. I am only glad she survived her foolishness."

"Well, John," stated Dr. Wills. "Lets see what we can do for this lass, okay? I'll have the orderlies move her to the operating room in the hospital."

"No, doctor, we must do it here!" Thunder stated firmly as he took hold of the doctor's arm. "Forgive me, Dr. Wills, Sir, but there are too many germs in there and I do not wish to move her."

"Well, then, John, you are on your own," The good doctor stated, feeling insulted. "But I will send for a surgical bag, and some whiskey."

While the doctor retrieved the items needed, John talked with the woman and her husband. He explained what he was going to do and why. The husband brushed his lips over his wife's, and with tears in his eyes said, "Do what you must, healer. She is my heart and soul and I will fight this big fight with you for her life."

CHAPTER 20: A NEW LIFE

Once the orderly returned with the supplies, John moved the woman outside the tent, where the sun could be best used as lighting. He knew he needed to work fast, because he only had two good hours of daylight left. There, on the ground, he built a small fire for the two knives he would use. He had obtained them from the women in the tent, and they were razor sharp. The orderly and a nurse brought up a table and set it up, then the nurse set about scrubbing and draping the young mother once she was placed upon it.

After that, John exposed the woman's belly. He took some soapy water and then cleansed her well a second time. Then he took the whiskey, and using a sponge made of clean, boiled cotton, he cleansed her belly once again. Afterward, he cleansed himself in the same manner. Dr. Wills watched John in wonder, but became beside himself when John took up the first knife and ran it through the fire several times, whispering his chanted prayers.

He calmed quickly as the first cut was made, precise and clean. The woman felt little pain, and because the knife was very hot, little blood was lost. The next knife cut was more difficult. John didn't want to break the woman's water with the next cut, so he asked a small girl of about ten winters to assist him. He found a slippery elm twig about twelve inches long prior to the orderly's arrival that he quickly pealed, and had notched it at one end. He gave it to the child now and instructed her how to pass it up into the woman's vagina to snag the mother's water bag and break it from there. By doing this, he felt that the infected fluids would drain out and away from the patient.

The girl washed well and after taking a deep breath, she reached up inside the woman and positioned the stick at the mouth of the woman's womb. John took up the second heated knife and took a deep breath, flashing the child a reassuring smile before he commanded, "NOW!"

John took the second heated knife and made the second cut just as the child broke the waters. Again, little blood was lost as the womb was opened. John then carefully reached his hand inside and carefully brought out the dead infant, which dripped jelly-like placenta. Laying the stillborn beside his mother, he turned back to suture her, but was stopped suddenly when he saw something move within her. He quickly asked the husband when his wife was due, and was relieved to find she was full term. John, smiling with wonder, reached back inside the woman, and with trembling hands, he very carefully withdrew a small, but healthy baby boy that started squalling spontaneously. He then tied off the cord and the father cut it.

John gave the infant over to an astonished Dr. Wills and returned to his patient. Dr. Wills started coaching John then about the best way to remove the next placenta to minimize blood loss, but John proved to be well up to the task. The nurse, whose name was Jones, started to hand him some cat gut suture when John frowned, and with a sharp voice, he commanded, "Wash first, and soak those in the whiskey! Then pass that needle through the fire three times!"

The nurse, Ms. Jones, blushed and stammered out a weak, "O... okay."

"Then do it! Do it now, and quickly!"

Just then, the little girl whose hand was still inside the woman's vagina, squealed, "She's bleedin', sir."

"Is it a lot, little one?"

The child looked at him with puzzlement, so Nurse Jones, feeling the need to redeem herself, looked under the blanket. "No, sir, t'is not abnormal."

"Good. Now, little one, I want you to push up inside the mother, slow and steady, while I finish the stitches, okay?"

The child did as she was asked, and John finished his stitching inside in record time. Once that was done, the child removed her small hand very slowly, and John watched as the womb collapsed in upon itself. He then took more sterile suture from the nurse and stitched up the abdominal muscles, and then the skin. While Thunder Heart washed up, Dr. Wills handed the babe to the mother, who held him weakly as tears of joy trickled from her fever-dulled eyes.

Thunder smiled as he dressed the woman's abdomen. Then, while he smoothed the hair from the young woman's brow, he stated in a soft and gentle voice, "He is small, but strong. I do not think the fever has harmed him, but he must not drink your milk until you have recovered."

The mother nodded as John wiped away her tears and, Nurse Jones, who also had tears in her eyes, said she would go find a wet nurse.

The woman's husband held out his hand to John and gave him a single grizzly bear claw. Thunder Heart took it reverently and asked, "What will you name your son?"

The woman shook her head and pointed to him. Thunder Heart dropped his head in humility. Then he stood, and picking up the small squalling infant into his large but gentle hands, he raised his head and eyes heavenward and sang out in Cheyenne, and then in English.

"I, oh *Maheo'o*, am Thunder Heart, He Who Walks With The White Buffalo, Healer and Singer of the Cheyenne people. See this small one whose heart was to strong to die. Bless him always, and know that from this day forward, unless you change it, he will be called by the people, "Strong Heart, He Who has the Heart of the Grizzly."

Then he handed the child to his father, who stated with a nod and a wave of his hand, "*Epeva'he'e* (it is good)."

Dr. Wills, shaking his head, came forward and slapped a firm hand on Thunder Heart's shoulder and said, "John, that was the finest piece of surgery I have ever seen. Have you any further experience with surgery?"

"Sir, thank you. I have done an appendectomy and aided in the removal and subsequent repair of several bullet wounds. Being a Cheyenne, you see, doctor," he chuckled, "Is a health hazard."

Dr. Wills let out a hearty laugh. "Well, my boy, I understand your point. Have you ever wanted to take the tests to become a legal doctor?"

"Sir, yes I have, and would like to do so, but do you really think I would be accepted by white men as a doctor the same as you are? To work in a fine hospital as you do?"

"My boy, you can work with me any day, but you're right. The rich folks would not accept you. But what about the poor, the Chinese, and the whores? They don't seek help here, and doctors are too few in the world."

Thunder Heart nodded thoughtfully. "Thank you, Dr. Wills. I will think seriously about it, but for now I need to get back to the boarding house and check on Mari. I'll be back tomorrow after we lay her brother to rest."

After instructing the family members of his patients how to care for them, and Nurse Jones how to administer the teas he had brewed, he wearily left by carriage for the hotel, calling over his shoulder for them to come and get him only if he were sorely needed.

CHAPTER 21: MITAWIN

Mari had slept on and off while Thunder Heart was away, and was now dressed and sitting in the rocking chair, staring out the window of her room when he returned. She looked so lost and alone sitting there with her handkerchief in her hand, that it made his heart break for her. He walked over to her, wrapping his arms protectively around her shoulders and whispered softly into her ear. "How do you feel, *mitawin*?"

Looking up at him, tears still streaking her cheeks, she asked,

"*Mitawin*? What does that mean?"

He dropped to his knees beside her. "*Mitawin*," he stated as he ran his fingers through her hair. "Means my woman, or wife, in the language of my people."

"W-wife?" she stammered looking at him with eyes as big as saucers.

"Yes. Wife. I am asking you to marry me, Mari. Today, as I helped save the life of a young mother and her child, I realized again how short and precious life is. So I want you to know that I do love you, and I can't imagine my life anymore without you."

She flung herself into his arms and with tears of joy streaming down her face, she shouted. "Oh, yes! Yes, John. I will marry you."

She kissed him as she wrapped her arms around his neck. He pulled her into his lap as he sat in the bedside chair and deepened their kiss. As he gently caressed her face, he whipped away her tears with his thumbs. She was so desirable, and his blood burned for her.

He yearned for the feel of her body beneath his. He wanted with all his being to feel her pulsating sheath surround him as he poured his life into her. But he knew it was too soon. He would not rush her with the heat of his passion. He wanted her to be sure she knew fully what a life with him would be before he took her to his bed. Her sacred gift could only be given once and he, feeling very selfish, wanted that gift to be his once and forever without any regret.

He continued to kiss her deeply, tasting her honeyed lips with his tongue until she parted them and allowed him entrance. Once there, he caressed her mouth fully with his until he had learned every nuance of it. Their tongues dueled, caressing each other before he began to thrust his tongue in and out as if he were making love to her.

She was becoming breathless and trembled in his arms. He stirred her soul to heights of such bliss that she thought she was drifting toward heaven itself. She could feel her blood burning within her veins, and she reached up and buried her slender fingers deep within his thick, ebony hair, pulling him closer. Moaning with desires she had never dreamed possible, she pulled back just enough to gaze into his smoldering blue eyes, and gasped when she saw the depth of his love within them. She lifted her hand to caress his face, and he let out a soft moan of pleasure as he continued to caress her arms and shoulders.

"John Thunder Heart, make love to me. Here, now, please."

He held her close and laid her head against his chest so she could hear his heart beating like a great drum within him. It took all his control to refuse her, but refuse her he did.

Caressing her, he stated softly, yet firmly, as he looked deeply into her passion filled eyes, "Mari, I want this gift you offer to me with all of my heart, but I will not take it before we are wed. To do so now would dishonor us both. You must also know that as a woman belonging to an Indian, you will suffer greatly at the hands of your people."

Mari, looking deeply into his eyes, clearly stated from her heart, "I don't care what others think about me. I'm honored to be loved by you, John."

"Thank you, Mari, but I do care what others would call you and how they will treat you. It is my wish to protect you from all hurt and cruelty. Please, for now, let me just hold you, my sweet, and tell you of my day."

The last rays of the setting sun streamed in through the smudged window, bathing them with its warmth as they sat on the bed, holding each other close. Thunder Heart stroked her auburn curls and spoke of his patients and how his surgical skill had impressed Dr. Wills and saved the life of the young wife and her babe.

"Mari, Dr. Wills said he thinks I should take the Board of Doctor's Exam to become a real paper-caring doctor like himself. Do you think this would be a good idea?"

Stunned that he would ask her what she thought, she pulled away from him and smiled as she took his large, capable hands in hers. Then taking a deep breath, she stated firmly, "That's so wonderful, and yes, John, I think you should. It would prove to my people that you really are a doctor in every way. Are you going to do it?"

"I told him I would like to do it, but that I feared that the good whites of this city would not want an Indian doctor taking care of them. Dr. Wills said the poor red, yellow and black people would not care. I will never become rich, Mari, but all I have would be yours."

Laying her head again over his heart she smiled. "I don't care about fancy things, John. Do you think I could train with you to become your helper?" She lifted her face to look into his deep blue eyes to gauge his response.

"Why, yes!" The excitement and joy of the moment rose within him and spilled out in his twinkling eyes and broad smile. Grabbing her by the shoulders, he stated, "Mari, that's a wonderful idea. I could have used your help even today. Tomorrow, after we have buried your brother, would you come with me to check on my patients?"

Mari swallowed and her eyes misted briefly. She had momentarily forgotten her brother in her joy over being loved, but then she remembered something her brother had said to her the first night on the ship as they left their old life behind: Be happy, Mari. The only happiness we have in life is what we make for ourselves, and I want you to be happy.

Blinking away her sadness, she beamed a radiant smile at John and stated with her whole heart, "Why, yes, John, I would love that. I think staying busy would be good for me right now anyway."

Later, after their supper, they spent the rest of their evening giving each other more tender kisses and caresses. Thunder thought, as he fought for control, that this was the sweetest of tortures.

As night fell, he was unable to leave her side, so he continued to read to her until she fell asleep, holding her close well into the night before he returned to his own bed.

The next morning, John and Mari, who was dressed in a black dress and veil that Billy Blue Hawk's mother had given her, walked to the undertaker's where they would board the carriage that would take them to the cemetery. It wasn't a long walk, but they had to pass by a rough-looking, loud saloon. The loggers had arrived last night from the camps, and were still drinking come morning. Several of those still-inebriated men sat in front of the saloon on the bench.

As John and Mari approached, the rude men began to cat call at Mari, and when John took her arm, steering her around them, he vaguely heard a profane remark about a stinking Indian and Mari being a whore. The gall rose within him, but he clenched his jaw and kept them walking. He would not fight today. Mari and his patients needed him.

The ride to the cemetery took about an hour, traveling on a well-worn road that traversed up a hilly trail surrounded by tall old growth trees dotted here and there with dogwoods and red buds. The ride would have been beautiful but for the trembling woman in his arms. Thunder tried talking to her and pointing out the forest's beauty as a way to get Mari to relax, and it did help some, but when they entered the glade in which stood an open grave, Mari broke down. She clung to him, weeping, and it took a while to walk her from the carriage to the grave sight.

Thunder then returned to help the driver, undertaker, and the preacher carry Robert's coffin to the grave. Once they had lowered him into the ground, he returned to Mari's side. She grabbed his hand and held it tightly as hot tears streamed down her pale cheeks. The Preacher read the twenty-third psalm and they all sang the old rugged cross. As the men started filling in the grave, Thunder began to sing in Cheyenne, and this alone comforted Mari more than anything else, because she knew that it came directly from his heart.

After the grave was closed, Thunder took Mari's hand and walked her back to the carriage. At this point, she didn't know what she felt anymore. She was so confused. All her emotions were so jumbled within her that when he lifted her up into the carriage and her eyes locked with his, he became her total focus. He was her family now, and Lord forgive her, but her thoughts kept going back to thoughts of his strong arms and what it would be like to be loved fully by him.

He sat down in the carriage beside her and she laid her head over onto his shoulder. Drying her face with her sleeve, she shuddered out a statement, "Thank you, John, for your song. What was it about?"

"It was a prayer, Mari. My people sing our prayers. We believe that singing is God's special language— the language of the soul. I was thanking *Ma'heo'o* for your brother's life and for bringing you to me. I also asked for *Ma'heo'o* to bring your brother peace in the knowledge that I will love you always and protect you with my life. I also told him he should walk the sky road with light steps knowing that you would be safe and well taken care of."

Tears filled her eyes again, and she hugged him, weeping with deep body-racking sobs. They were the kind of tears that cleansed the heart and soul, and by the time the carriage pulled up in front of the boarding house, her emotions were no longer mixed up. She felt like she had been made anew, and only joy and love remained inside. When she went to get out of the carriage, the world spun and she fainted. John reacted quickly, sweeping her up into his arms and carried her into the hotel.

Once inside, he carried her right up to her room and laid her upon the bed. He quickly loosened her corset, and using some smelling salts from his bag, he slowly revived her.

"John, what happened?" she asked as she gasped for breath.

"You fainted, Mari. You haven't eaten much of late, so I think you should rest a while."

"But we have to change and eat before we go to the hospital and check on your patients, right?"

"Do you think you'll feel up to it today, Mari?"

"Oh, yes, John. I'll take off this corset and eat some of Nelly's stew and I'll feel right as rain again. Besides, my brother would be the first to say that life must go on and your patients need you. Helping you will make me happy."

Nelly, hearing that her favorite tenants had returned, came into the foyer. Wiping her hands on her apron, she looked up the stairs and said loudly, "Come on into me dinin' room, you two! I have some stew and biscuits made for ye!"

Mari, feeling much better once she had changed her clothes, hurried down the stairs and hugged the elderly woman, telling her she was starved. John just smiled and told Nelly that everything went well at the gravesite, and that after Mari had a good cry, she felt much relieved.

CHAPTER 22: WHITE MAN'S HATE

Radner Jones was one of the many loggers who had come from the east to find their fortune. He had been at the local logging camp for almost a year now, and like many of the men, he came into town on pay day to drink and visit the whores.

He personally had traveled to the great northwest in search of gold. He met up with his friend Zeke in the gold fields. After spending too many cold, wet days with little to show for their efforts, they decided over a cheap bottle of red eye to try logging instead. The great Northwest had taught them one of life's simple truths: If you want a steady supply of liquor, you needed a steady supply of money.

Radner wasn't a very good logger. He was lazy and took short cuts often, felling trees too close to other men. He enjoyed watching them run for their lives. He also hated Indians because he had lost his parents and little sister some years back, when some renegades attacked their wagon train. So, after seeing how the logging bosses used the local Indians to tag trees for cutting and other jobs, he decided to take his revenge out on them by arranging accidents.

Everyone knew that cutting trees was a real hazard that all the men faced each day. No one said anything when a few Indians were hurt or killed, and with each death that he made happen, Radner's massive, oversized ego grow even bigger.

Today he and Zeke sat in front of the Red Bird Saloon, nursing a hangover, when he saw an Indian wearing a white man's clothing, carrying the most beautiful white woman he had ever seen. He watched them go toward the Hotel, and stated while absentmindedly rubbing his crotch, "Zeke you sees what I see?"

"Yea Rad, a stinkin' injun with his hands on a white woman. He's too uppity, that one. It ain't right, Rad. It ain't right."

"No, it ain't right," Rad stated with a sneer on his lips and his eyes blazing with hate.

Radner and Zeke followed John and Mari and watched as they entered the Hotel. Radner rubbed his face and scratched his filthy red beard thoughtfully.

"Zeke, let's just watch these two for a while, and then catch um one night in the dark. We could take em in that alley over there behind the saloon and have us a little fun. Waddya think, Zeke?"

Zeke spit on the street and wiped the tobacco juice from his mouth with the back of his dirt-encrusted hand before stating, "Yeah, Rad. she's too good fir the likes of him, but not too good fir us. Let's go. I needs me another drink."

As they turned to leave, Radner spotted Billy Blue Hawk coming out of the Hotel. He grabbed the boy, jerking him hard to face him, and commanded that he tell him who the woman and Indian were who just went into the Hotel.

Billy's mouth went dry. He swallowed several times before he could get the words out, but as the big logger shook him, he raised his chin and stated proudly, "That there be Dr. John Thunder Heart and Miss Mari. They live here. Her brother died in dat storm we had and they buried him today."

Radner released Billy, shoving him face-first into the dirt and laughed as the child scrambled to his feet and took off running toward the back of the hotel. Then he and Zeke sauntered back to the Saloon where they could sit and keep watch. Later that day, they saw Billy hold the horses for Thunder as he helped Mari get into a carriage. Once Thunder climbed in, Billy released the team and stood there waving as they rode away.

"Zeke, go ask dat kid again where they be off to."

Zeke left and came back quickly to tell Radner that the kid said they were going to the hospital and would be back at sundown.

Radner smiled wickedly, and while rubbing his crotch, he said, "Well, Zeke, ain't that just wonderful? Let's go and have us sum beer and play cards. Someday we's gonna have us sum poon and beat us an uppity Injun."

CHAPTER 23: MUCH WORK TO DO

After a delicious meal, they went upstairs and changed. Mari did away with the black dress for a plain gray one she had bought the day before. John, thinking that it was a good idea to continue dressing like a white man while at the hospital, but wanting to be more comfortable, removed his suit jacket and tie and left them on the chair in his room. An hour later, they rode through the busy streets, paying no attention to the pointing and snide comments of the onlookers, until they arrived at the hospital where they were met by Dr. Wills.

"Well, well, my boy, I'm so glad to see you. Did you decide to take the Doctor's Exam?"

"Yes, he has," Mari piped up excitedly. "And I have decided to train to be his nurse."

Thunder Heart chuckled softly, shaking his head.

"Yes, doctor, it seems that my Mari is already behaving like a wife, and speaking for me."

Dr. Wills' entire face showed his shock. "You asked her to marry you, John?"

"Yes, doctor." He passed Mari a quick glance. "I feel, however, that we should wait for a while before we wed. I want her to be really sure what her life will be like marring an Indian before we set a date."

"Dr. Wills," Mari giggled girlishly. "Don't let John fill you with his worries. I truly love him and my feelings are not going to change. I want us to marry just as soon as he passes his tests."

"Well, my dear," replied the nervous doctor. "That sounds like a plan. But for now, we have patients to see."

Thunder helped Mari down from the carriage, and they walked out from under the hospital's grand awning and into the bright, warm sunshine. The ferocious storm had swept Old Man Winter away, leaving behind clean, warm air that smelled of ocean spray and fresh earth.

The tents that housed the many people injured by the storm were beginning to thin out as families took their loved ones home, and even though there were beds inside the hospital, the poor could not enter. Mari was shocked by how many patients were crowded into the small tents, but Thunder was not. He greeted them all with a warm, confident smile. Mari observed that John was in his element here, commanding the respect of all, even the hospital staff, as he directed them in ways to help. She was standing back, out of the way and observing, when two elderly Indian people approached John.

He greeted them warmly and enfolded the elderly woman, who was wearing a sling on her splinted arm, in a tender hug. He even placed a kiss upon her forehead before stating, "It is good to see you doing so well, Grandmother and Grandfather Walking Bear. Have our people been treated well?"

The elder's face looked stern and he spoke softly. "We have not had enough to eat and we still have not received enough blankets and wood to keep the weak ones warm."

John's blood started to boil, and he called Mari forward. "Everyone, this is Mari. She too has survived the great storm, and is now here to learn the ways of helping." Everyone nodded politely to her. Mari blushed and smiled weakly before dropping her head, reminded again of her losses.

"Mari, I need you to take Walking Bear to the general store. The one beside the bank. Use Dr. Wills' buggy, okay? Once there, you will give this note…" He reached into his pocket and handed her a folded piece of paper. "…To the store keeper. Then I want you to buy all the tin cups, bowls, spoons, and blankets he has. I also want you to buy some dried beef, potatoes, onions, a sack of oats, ground corn, salt, and sugar. And oh, a pot of honey also."

"Okay, John. We will hurry back as quickly as possible."

After Mari and Walking Bear had hurried out of the tent, Dr Wills stepped up to John as he was restarting the fire in the small central stove.

"John, you're buying these things out of your own pocket?"

John straightened and looked at the doctor squarely. "I am a healer, sir. I am here to serve them, not to profit from their suffering. All God has given me— my life, my mind, my hands, and yes, my money— was given to me so that I may serve them. This is where the Indian and the whites differ. If I were ill, my people would heal me. If I were hungry, cold, or in need of shelter, they would gladly provide it. In this, doctor, I am a very rich man indeed."

"I meant no disrespect, John. I was just worried whether you had enough money to buy everything that you wanted. I was going to pitch in some of my own money as well."

John took a deep breath, letting the anger flow from him, and calmly said, "Thank you, sir. I am sorry I took offense. But don't worry. I have more than enough money to provide for my patients needs."

They had completed their rounds of the Indian tent and were heading over to the Chinese tent when Mari and Walking Bear returned. Dr. Wills grabbed a wandering orderly and assigned him to unloading the supplies and placing them into the Indian tent before he went to gather enough wood for all the tents. Dr. Wills told the man that he was now personally responsible for keeping the firewood stacked high beside each tent, and if he did not, he would be out of a job. The man flushed red before answering in a shaking voice, "Yes sir, doctor, sir. I'll get right to it."

Once the supplies were unloaded, Mari went about passing out cups, bowls, and blankets to all the patients while the female family members started preparing a large pot of stew over a fire they had built outside the tent. Inside, Mari heated a large pot of water on the now-glowing Ben Franklin for John's teas, and started a small pot of broth and corn gruel for the more seriously ill patients.

When she was done there, she went to the other tents, distributing blankets, utensils, and food where it was needed. She finally caught up with John at the tent that housed the soiled doves. John shook his head when he saw their sorry state. No one had aided them or even brought their needs to Dr. Wills' attention. Many wore only their undergarments and suffered from fevers, fractures, and pneumonia. All John had to do was look at Mari, and she was off, gathering everything she needed to make them more comfortable. When she was running across the hospital grounds, she met up with a minister making his rounds.

"Kind sir, could I speak to you?"

"Why, yes, my dear child."

As she worried the small apron she wore to hide her trembling hands, she humbly asked, "Sir, is there any way that you could help me obtain some dresses for the doves? I, ah, mean working ladies in yonder tent? It is most unseemly for them to wander about in their underwear."

The minister thought for a moment, then after scratching his chin, he said confidently and without disdain, "My wife and the good ladies of our congregation gathered donations from the townspeople right after the storm hit. I'm heading home for lunch as we speak. When I get there, I will have my wife get right on it and I'll have the things with me when I return."

"Oh, thank you, pastor," Mari gushed, a smile brightening her lovely face. "My John will be most pleased to have a man of faith willing to aid his patients."

Later that evening, the pastor returned just as he had promised and brought four boxes of clothing for the ladies. Mari was so excited, but the good reverend was taken aback by the conditions within the hospital tents and was even more so by the fact that their physician was an Indian. When Dr. Wills saw how the man dropped the boxes and started heading right back to his carriage, he decided to stop him.

"Excuse me Reverend, but is there something wrong? Mari told us that you would be ministering to the patients while you were here."

"Sir, how can you of all people allow that heathen to act like a doctor for those poor folks? I intend to address this with your superiors."

"Well, you can do that if you like reverend, but I am the head of this hospital. As far as that heathen, as you call him, his name is John Thunder Heart and he is the finest young doctor I have ever had the privilege to work with. If you would, sir, just take the time to really observe him taking care of his patients. You'll see how wrong you are. Please come back with me to the tent and watch for a while before you judge him so harshly."

The Reverend took a deep breath and followed Dr. Wills back to the ladies tent.

Once inside, he did indeed observe a kind and competent doctor who brewed up his own medicines and taught others how to administer them.

Finally, John took a break and noticed the reverend who watched his approach with apprehension in his eyes. John held out his hand, and smiling, stated, "Thank you for coming, reverend. As you can see, your congregation's donations were sorely needed and greatly appreciated.

While I can attend to the physical and emotional needs of these patients, I am ill-equipped to aid them spiritually. As you can see, it is the women in our world who suffer the most. Uneducated and unable to find benefactors, they are forced to sell the only thing they own: their bodies, to keep themselves alive. Did you know that many of them are mothers and Christians, but they told me that they are not welcome in any of the churches in town? I have told them that Jesus still loves them, and has not forsaken them because of how they live. I told them that as long as they had faith in him that nothing could keep them out of the kingdom of heaven and that their sins were forgiven from the moment of his sacrifice on the cross."

The reverend shook his head and gave an astounded look to Dr. Wills before he took John's hand and shook it firmly. "Dr. John Heart, you are truly a remarkable man. You said you were ill-equipped to help these people spiritually, but you underestimate yourself, sir. Never have I heard the salvation message put better, and I am truly pleased to make your acquaintance."

After that, the reverend introduced himself to everyone as Pastor Johnson, and he did finally decide to sit for quite a while, talking and praying with many of the patients. It was becoming quite late, and John could see that Mari was getting very tired, but they needed to check in on one other patient in the Chinese tent before they left for the night.

Dr. Wills had been using a young man named Woo Lee as his translator, and expressed to him that John was in need of more herbal medicines.

Woo Lee said he would arrange it.

When John and Mari arrived at the Chinese tent, they were met by a small, white-haired man who bowed low before he introduced himself as Mr. Wong Lee.

"Doctor, I am very happy and grateful to meet you. My grandson has spoken highly of you and I have sampled your teas, and have found them to be very good, but you are running low. Are you not?"

Thunder took the elder's hand, and looking the man in the eyes and seeing no deceit there, stated, "Thank you, Grandfather Lee for your praise. I am indeed running low on many of my herbs. Do you know where I may go to replace them?"

"Yes, doctor. I am a medicine maker for my people. I have a shop filled with herbs. My people come to me and they tell me how they feel, and I give them the right herbs to heal them. Rarely do they need more help than that. If you would come with me after you are through for the day, I will take you to my store and we will get all the things you require."

"Thank you, sir," Thunder said. "Let me check on these patients and we can be on our way."

Thunder hurriedly, yet carefully checked on all the patients there, and sent many of them home, but there was one special case yet to see. A small boy who's leg had had a severe compound fracture. John had set the bone and sutured the leg, but he was worried that infection would set in. When he checked on him, he found the child much improved. The leg was healing well, and the boy showed no signs of fever. His family had faithfully followed Thunder's instructions to the letter. So with a happy heart, he pronounced the child fit to be sent home but only after he instructed the family how and when to use the new medicine he provided. He also informed them that if they had further need of him, to contact Mr. Lee and he would come right away.

The sun was setting when John, Mari, Mr. Lee and his grandson left the hospital grounds for the apothecary shop. As they rode through the ever-increasingly narrow streets, Thunder was awestruck by the foreignness of the area. The buildings were jammed so close together, he didn't see how anyone could fit between them. There was a beautifully-decorated building painted brightly and accented by gold colored dragons. When they finally arrived at Mr. Lee's shop and entered, Thunder's jaw dropped. It was like no other store he had ever been in. This was part of a world totally foreign to him, and he felt like a child as he feasted his eyes on the wonders before him. There were jars and paper packages stacked high on shelves that covered the walls floor to ceiling. The smell of burning incense filled his nose and the tinkling of glass chimes filled his ears and he found the store very soothing to the soul.

The shop was an herbalist's dream. Everything he needed, he found, and even though the names were different for each herb, Mr. Lee could recognize it from its taste or smell alone.

John could have spent hours talking to Mr. Lee, but it was late and Mari was worn out. So, with his medicine bag fully restocked, he bid Mr. Lee good night, and he and Mari headed back to the Hotel for a hot meal, a warm bath, and a soft bed.

CHAPTER 24: MUCH WORK TO DO

The next few weeks went by in a blur of working and studying.

The hospital tents were empty now, Mari was assigned to other patients to complete her training under Nurse Jones, and Thunder followed Dr. Wills while he did his rounds. Their days were filled with laughter and work, and their nights were filled with study and kisses. Thunder couldn't wait to make Mari fully his, but even though Mari continued to say she had no worries about being his bride, he did, and never let their desires go to completion.

The day of John's big test came in a rush of frantic studying and secrets.

Thunder headed off to Dr. Wills' office to take the test while Mari stayed at the Hotel. She was planning a picnic for them when he returned, and later she hoped to give him a very special gift.

Dr. Wills had no doubt that John would pass the test with flying colors, but Thunder had to take several deep breaths to calm his racing heart and focus on the questions at hand. After two hours, he finished and laid the test paper on the doctor's desk. Dr. Wills shook Thunder's hand and said, "Well, my boy we'll know by the end of the week if you passed or not, but as for myself, I have no doubts that you passed. Would you and Mari have dinner at my house on Saturday after next? I have some people who would love to meet you, and oh yes, it's going to be formal. Suits and such. Is that okay?"

"Yes, doctor. We'll be there, and formal wear will be fine. Then he smiled a devilish grin. "White man's formal, or beads-and-feathers formal?"

Dr. Wills snuck out an easy chuckle. "White man's… indeed. A suit will be fine my boy. I don't want my misses to faint before she gets to meet you, or the gardener to shoot you before you reached the door. We'll expect you both at two. Now off with you, son. Mari told Nurse Jones she had a surprise waiting for you.

Thunder shook the doctor's hand again and left at a jog, his imagination racing. When he arrived at the hotel, Mari greeted him with a bright smile and a picnic basket in her hand. Once again he was taken aback by her beauty. Dressed in a yellow gingham dress with her hair tied back with a matching ribbon, he felt she looked like pure sunshine.

"Well, well," he stated, smiling. "I see you have planned a picnic for us.

Where would you like to go?"

"Let's go get the carriage and go to the meadow that overlooks the bay. There are things we need to discuss."

"Yes, there are some very important things we need to discuss," he replied as he fingered the small box he had in his pants pocket. He had stopped off at the jeweler's shop on the way home and figured that today would be a good day to give it to her.

Hand-in-hand, they walked down the street to the livery again, unmindful of the vulgar talk aimed at them from the drunken loggers outside the Red Bird Saloon. Radner and Zeke had been playing cards and drinking all day with a bank teller that informed them that an uppity Indian had deposited a large amount of gold in his bank. This set Radner to a slow boil. He knew just which Indian it was and he planned on teaching him to mind his place.

John was all Cheyenne, but here in this place with Mari, he found it easy to fit into the white world, wearing white man's clothing and shoes, hiding his long hair. Yet deep in Thunder Heart's soul, he knew he didn't belong in this world, and longed to return home to his family and Mist Valley.

Once at the livery, Thunder helped Mr. Olson, the liveryman, to hitch up a small buck board for them. He placed the basket in the back and after he helped Mari to board, he climbed up beside her. He smiled down into her eyes for a heartbeat, then snapped the reigns and yelled, "Giddy up!"

The day was glorious, bright, sunny, and warm making the trip very enjoyable. After thirty minutes, they arrived at their destination.

The Meadow was beautiful, filled with new green grass and wild flowers. Mari spread a blanket on the hillock overlooking the bay, a good spot where they could watch the sailing ships and hear the gulls and crashing waves. Their meal was a simple one: fried chicken, biscuits, cheese and apple pie washed down with a small bottle of red wine. When they were done eating, Mari packed everything away and they sat with their arms around each other, watching the breaching whales in the bay.

"Mari, do you still want to be my wife?"

"Why, yes, John with all of my heart."

"You know that your life with me and my people will not be like it is here. We wear different clothing, live in simpler houses, and eat different foods. We even worship God differently than the whites do, but most of all many white people will treat you without respect because you are with me."

Mari turned toward him and took his face in her small hands.

She looked directly into those deep blue eyes of his before saying, "Listen to me, John Thunder Heart." It was the first time she had called him by his full name. "I love you. All of you. This means I love who you are inside and out. Your people will be my people and wherever and however we live will be wonderful because I'll be with you. I knew you weren't going to stay here, and I am looking forward to becoming your wife and going to live with your people."

Thunder Heart looked at her with such tenderness then that it brought tears to her eyes. He took her hands in his and kissed them before he reached into his right pants pocket and withdrew a small velvet box. Mari's eyes grew round and filled with tears upon seeing it, and she raised her fingers to her trembling lips.

"Mari, will you marry me in the white man's way?"

She extended her left hand and trembled as he placed the tiny garnet ring on her finger. "OH YES, John!" she shouted. "I will marry you any way you want, Indian or white."

She flung herself into his arms then, and he kissed her deeply. She tasted so sweet. He darted his tongue forward, parting her lips, and she opened them fully to allow his tongue to caress hers. He laid her gently back onto the blanket and continued the kiss. She was becoming breathless and lightheaded as her heart raced and her mind was filled with wanton yearnings she didn't understand. She pressed her body closer to his and he gasped as he felt her nipples harden as they touched his chest. He entwined his fingers in her silken hair, freeing it to tumble about her shoulders, then he ran his fingers down her cheek to her neck and across her collar bone to her breasts. She gasped as his fingers reached inside her bodice. She broke the kiss, arching her body to meet his touch, and she breathlessly begged, "Make love to me, John. Please."

John wanted her so badly, he hurt, but he would wait till their wedding night. For now, he would give her the first climax of her life. He reached down and caressed her leg, stroking it softly, gradually inching up her thigh under her skirt to caress her woman's mound. Not wanting to be separated from her body by her cotton underwear, he pulled the string and reached inside. She held tight to his broad shoulders and shuddered as he smoothed his fingers down the soft curls at the juncture of her legs, and she gasped when he parted her folds to caress the bud of her desire with a single calloused finger. With a repetitive circular motion, he rapidly caressed, all the while watching her face as he brought her closer to fulfillment. Then as she began to shudder, he kissed her deeply and sent her flying to the stars in his arms.

Gasping for breath, she clung to him until her body stopped shuddering. When she found her voice again, she said, "Oh, John, I never knew anyone could feel such pleasure. I felt like my heart was soaring to the heavens. Oh my, that was wonderful."

Thunder chuckled as he continued to hold her and stated, "*Meoon* (sweetheart), I will give you such pleasures when you are fully mine that it will make this one hardly worth remembering."

Mari didn't know what to say to that. All she could do was blush and giggle.

They continued to enjoy each other for a while longer, talking about many things. They even talked about weddings and how the white people's church differed from the Indian wedding of the moon. They strolled through the meadow, talking while Mari picked flowers. After which they returned to the blanket again where John took her into his arms and again brought her to climax, but the air was beginning to cool and he didn't know how much longer he could resist from taking her. They packed up their things and headed back to the hotel. Mari was lost in the afterglow of John's touch and her mind wandered to thoughts of her wedding night. John too was deep in thought, forgetting the dangers that lurked in this fancy world.

It was after dark when they dropped off the wagon at the livery and started walking back to the Hotel, but just before they reached there, they stopped in the shadow of the ally. Mari put her arms around his neck as John pulled her into his arms. He kissed her, gently caressing her neck and sliding his fingers up into her hair, holding her lips tenderly to his.

"Ne'me'hota'tse," he whispered in her ear.

She tenderly caressed his face with her long, slender fingers before she pulled him closer to her to deepen their kiss. Breathless, they finally broke their kiss and Mari stated, "Oh, John, my heart can't hold all the love I have for you. I finally feel I belong to life again because I belong with you."

As they were gazing deeply into each other's eyes, they didn't notice the spectators that were coming down the alley way toward them. The loud, bawdy music of the saloon masked their approach, enabling the drunken men to sneak up behind the loving couple.

Radner came up behind John and struck him hard on the head with a beer bottle just as Zeke grabbed Mari, covering her mouth with a filthy, dirt-encrusted, beefy hand, effectively silencing the attack.

John collapsed to the ground, blood pouring from a huge gash on the back of his head. Mari, fearing for John's life, struggled against the vice grip of the man who held her. Sickened and overwhelmed by the stench of the drunken unwashed man, she desperately tried to hold down the bile that rose within her throat. She kicked, scratched, and struggled with all her might to free herself, but in the end, she could do nothing but watch as Radner grabbed John by his boots, dragging him further behind the building where he began kicking, punching, and stomping on him.

NO! Mari's mind screamed, and Zeke began to tire of holding her. She became a hell cat, kicking and scratching as the adrenaline surged within her. She bit deeply into Zeke's hand, and for a brief moment, his hand loosened and she was able to let out an ear splitting scream. Radner, feeling he had adequately punished the Indian enough, came back to help his friend by back-handing Mari so hard she crumpled.

Once she was on the ground and at their mercy, Radner and Zeke forgot about Thunder Heart. They ripped open her bodice and chemise, sending tiny buttons flying into the air, and began roughly groping her breasts. They hiked up her skirt, viciously ripped off her bloomers, and began sticking their dirty fingers into her most private parts. She moaned, and just when she was about to let out another scream, Radner's fist smashed into her face, sending her once again into darkness.

Her right eye was swelling and turning blue as they ripped open the rest of her garments from her still form. Both men stood there for a few minutes raking her naked form with their lecherous eyes. Zeke started to drool.

"Let me have her, Rad. She's got the perdiest tits I ever did see."

Radner shoved his smaller partner away and hissed, "You hold her. I've worked hard for this poon."

Grabbing her ankles, Radner viciously yanked her legs apart, freed himself from his pants, and poised himself over her. He was ready to plunge into her innocent flesh with his huge, bulbous manhood, when Thunder Heart came to. Thunder's body was racked with pain as he stumbled to his feet, but it was quickly forgotten when he saw his sweet Mari about to be raped. With a soul filled with rage, he rose to his full height and charged forward. He was no longer John the doctor, he was Thunder Heart the warrior, and he would defend his woman with his life.

Gazing quickly around the garbage-strewn alleyway, he spied a loose two-by-four. Snatching it up as he ran, he took advantage of his enemy's distraction, and smashed Radner upside the head with it, effectively knocking him from Mari. Then he bashed Zeke with the back swing. Thunder, unable to catch his breath, sank to his knees, his head hanging and his body a mass of overwhelming pain.

Mari came to just then, and feeling her freedom, scrambled to her feet. Forgetting her nudity, she also grabbed herself a board and went to work on the two men, striking them repeatedly while shouting, "Take that you bastard pieces of shit!"

Just then the bar keep came out of the back door of the saloon to empty a spittoon, and upon seeing Mari with her dress ripped open and flailing away on two now unconscious men yelled, "Ma'am, I'll send for the Constable."

Mari relaxed then and replied breathlessly, as she pulled her torn dress around her, "Thank you, kind sir, these men attacked us and tried to kill us."

Searching around in the dim light, she saw Thunder struggling for breath as he knelt with his hands resting on his knees. Mari, spitting blood and dirt from her mouth, rushed to him and collapsed at his side, her legs shaking so badly they could no longer support her.

"Oh my God, John, you're hurt so bad," she choked out past her swollen, split lips. She caressed his blood-streaked face with trembling fingers, but Thunder couldn't reply. With great effort, he reached out and pulled her to him. She held him tenderly and wept, her tears streaking her bloodied face.

The barkeep came outside just then and upon seeing the men he had kicked out of his bar earlier, muttered some well-deserved cuss words. He retrieved some rope he had hanging nearby and quickly tied the unconscious men up. With that done, he came over to John and Mari, and thrusting out a huge paw stated, "Here you two, let me helps ya to the hotel. Name's Sam, Sam Beecher." Sam was a huge bear of a man who had no trouble assisting both John and Mari by putting one big beefy arm around each of them, practically carrying them both across the street. Once inside the hotel, Sam yelled for help.

"Ho, the house. I gots wounded here and they needs help fast!"

Nelly, her husband, Billy and his mother came rushing out into the lobby. Nelly gasped, "Miss Mari and Dr. Heart. Oh, me God! Take em up stairs, Mr. Beecher, first room on the right. And Billy, you go fetch that Dr. Wills them twos been workin' for."

Sam piped up, also asking Billy to bring the Constable back as well.

Billy ran out the door and right straight to the livery. Billy told Mr. Olson, the liveryman, what had happened and asked him to fetch the Constable for him while he fetched the doctor. Extremely upset that this should happen to two of the nicest people he'd ever met, Mr. Olson gladly complied, giving Billy his fastest horse to ride, also providing him with directions to the doctor's house. Nelly's hired help got John and Mari into their rooms and onto their beds where the two women preceded to undress and cover them to await the doctor's arrival.

The Constable arrived at the saloon post haste, and Sam helped him put Radner and Zeke into the jail. Sam gave the law-keeper a full report of what had happened, even adding how he had overheard

Radner bragging earlier before he tossed them out; how he had killed some Indians at the logging camp last week by dropping a tree on their heads. Sam couldn't stomach those two, and he hoped they'd hang for what they had done.

CHAPTER 25: PAIN AND SUFFERING

Nelly cradled a sobbing Mari in her arms, rocking her gently. "Nelly, it was so awful," whimpered Mari. "When John didn't fight back after a while, I thought that filthy gutter rat had killed him. I tried to fight, Nelly, really I did."

"Now, now, there child, I know you did."

"But the big man hit me, and then I felt like I was far away, watching everything. I wanted to throw up. God, Nelly they tore my clothes and poked into me."

She trembled anew and sobbed great soul-wrenching sobs, wetting Nelly's shoulder with her tears. "John, John! Nelly I've got to go to him. He's hurt, bad."

"Stay here, child. "

She started to get up, but Nelly pushed her back onto the bed, saying, "He's out cold, hun. Billy's gone to fetch the doctor. You rest while I draw you up a hot bath and get you presentable, okay? Then you can go to him." Mari nodded and curled into a ball under the covers, hugging her pillow tight to her chest. She wanted to close her eyes and rest, but her mind kept playing and replaying the horrible events in her mind. She was sick with worry about Thunder. She kept seeing that man kicking and yelling filthy names at him, saying he was going to kill him for ever thinking he was good enough to have a white woman. Fearful that Thunder would turn on her and blame her for his misfortune, she started weeping anew. In a matter of weeks, she had lost everything, and John Thunder Heart was all she had left in the world.

"Oh, God, she prayed. "Don't let him die. I can't loose him, too. Oh God, don't let him stop loving me. PLEASE, I can't live without him!"

By the time Dr. Wills arrived, both Thunder heart and Mari had been bathed and made comfortable. Dr. Wills rushed into John's room to find Mari dressed in her night rail and wrapper, sitting in a chair beside the bed, weeping and holding John's swollen hand.

Dr. Wills shook his head as he took in, at a glance, the condition of the young couple. Mari was covered with bruises and abrasions. Her right eye nearly swollen shut. John was so badly beaten it made him almost unrecognizable. But it was when Dr. Wills pulled back the covers and saw the deep bruises to John's sides, torso, and abdomen that his heart lurched. Galvanized by anger, the doctor went to work, taking off his coat and rolling up his sleeves. While washing his hands using the bowl and pitcher from the wash stand, he started issuing orders.

"Ms. Nelly, fetch me all the ice you have. Have your husband smash it and bring it up here right away. I'll also need towels and clean muslin to use as bandages. If you have to, go to the store. Tell them to put it all on my bill. Now hurry, please!"

Mari looked up at Dr. Wills, tears trickling down her bruised cheeks, her lips swollen and trembling, eyes sad and beseeching. "Please, Dr. Wills, you have to help him. It's all my fault, sir. I shouldn't have kissed him in public. Oh, GOD, PLEASE! I can't lose him, too."

Dr. Wills gently wiped away her tears with gentle hands and placed a fatherly kiss on her forehead.

"Relax child. Let me look him over, okay?"

"That man beat him so bad. He hit him in the head first, knocking him out. I thought he'd killed him, there was so much blood. Then the smaller man grabbed me from behind and I watched as the big man punched and kicked and stomped on John. I fought really hard, but that's when he started hitting me too."

"Mari, do you know how long John was knocked out for?"

"I don't know, really. Maybe about five or ten minutes, but he got up and saved me by bashing them both before they raped me good. He was gasping for breath after that and passed out again after we got here."

While Mari had been talking, Wills had been assessing John's condition. His condition was grave. He had a severe concussion and several broken ribs, as well as bruising to his kidneys, spleen and liver. His face also sported a broken nose and possibly a fractured jaw bone. Wills marveled at how John could have overcome the pain at all to help Mari, but then love could make any man into a true hero when need be.

When Nelly returned with the muslin, Dr. Wills set about binding Thunder Heart's ribs. Then he took the ice Nelly had brought, wrapped it in towels and placed them on his abdomen. With Nelly's help, he raised John's head and shoulders up to reduce the brain swelling and to help him breathe better. Then he placed cold packs to his head and face.

"Well," Dr. Wills stated. "All we can do now is hope and pray that I don't have to operate on him. Mari, do you know where John's herbs are?"

Startled, she said, "Ah, ah yes. He keeps them in his bag over there." She was mentally shutting down. Wills realized she was going into shock.

"Nelly, help me get her into her bed so I can examine her, and then can you go and fetch me a teapot of hot water to make her some tea in."

Nelly did as she was asked and fled quickly to get the teapot. Mari stared at the ceiling as Dr. Wills examined her entire body. The worst of her injuries were her black eye and possible fractured jaw. She also had some vaginal bleeding. Wills shook his head at the brutality of those filthy-minded men.

She was cut and bruised, and they had even torn her maiden head with their violent probing. Wills placed a wad of gauze between her legs to staunch the bleeding before covering her up. He shook his head, thinking that if those men recovered from their injuries, they should be hung for what they had done to these precious young people.

Nelly returned with the teapot and Dr. Wills mixed up the relaxing tea blend of herbs that John had taught him about.

"Ms. Nelly, thank you for all your help this night." Handing her the teapot, he requested wearily, "Try to get her to drink some of this and keep applying the cold compresses to her face. Tomorrow I want her to soak in a hot salt water bath. We need to soak out the filth those bastards put in her."

Nelly blanched, and putting her hand to her heart, said, "Oh me God, the poor wee thing. Don't you be frettin' none, sir, I'll be tending this wee one all night."

Dr. Wills nodded and returned to Thunder Heart's side. Taking John's pulse and respiration again, and noting them to still be within normal limits, he sat down in the soft floral chair beside the bed. He sighed, cleaned his glasses and picked up a book from the bedside table and began to read.

He had heard of the tale of Moby Dick but had never read the book. Now he guessed he would get the chance. The next few hours were critical and he needed to stay awake. After a while, Nelly brought him a cup of coffee before returning to sit with Mari.

Mari slept fitfully, waking often in fear and calling John's name. Each time, Nelly was there to calm her and lovingly encourage her to drink her tea. Finally Dr Wills, heartsick by the way Mari was mentally suffering, gave her some laudanum to help her sleep.

At day break Nelly left to fix breakfast for the hotel's guests and said she would send Billy up with some food for them too.

Thunder Heart drifted in a mist of pain. The blackness hovered over him like a predator and he wished it would just get it over with and take him, but out of the painful mist that surrounded him appeared the White Buffalo.

It stood before him as it had in visions past and spoke with a thunderous voice, "Thunder Heart of the Cheyenne. Does your heart still not beat with mine? The *washitu* (white man) have caused you great hurt, but your suffering is nothing compared to that of the people. You can not live in the world of the white man. Your destiny is with your own kind. Learn and go home my brother."

After the buffalo left him, the mist lifted and he walked in the sun-warmed valley of his youth. This was his world. His home; a place of beauty not devoid of dangers, but this world he understood. He lay down under an old cottonwood that grew near the river, and while closing his eyes, he focused on the sounds of the birds and rushing river. He rested there, warm and safe without pain, comforted by Mother Earth and Father Sky.

It was around dawn when Dr. Wills noticed that John's breathing had become more relaxed and his color improved. The blueness from his lips was gone, and the bruising to his abdomen was unchanged.

Dr. Wills patted John's hand. "Good, son," he said. "You're a fighter. Sleep on, even though I would like for you to awaken, nothing but pain awaits you here. And oh, by the way, Mari's okay. We're taking good care of her, and those bastards who attacked you are lying miserable in the city jail."

Dr. Wills shook his head. He didn't usually talk to his unconscious patients. He guessed he was just tired, but afterward, he noticed that John's muscles and hands relaxed finally, along with his breathing.

Dr. Wills sat back down in the chair made some notes in his journal and drifted off to sleep.

It was after dark the next day when Thunder Heart and Mari returned to the world of the living. Wills and Nelly had worked tirelessly over their charges and were pleased to see them awaken, but they had their hands full calming them down.

Mari woke up first in a panic, sweating and trembling. "John! John!" She shouted. "I have to see John!"

Nelly rushed to her side and hugged her close. "Now there, there, me child, it will be okay now. Dr. Wills has been takin' care of him all the while."

"But I have to see him, Nelly, Please!"

"Okay child, okay. You can be goin' to see em, but after your bath. Dr. Wills said you had to soak a while to wash away what dem evil bastards did to ya, okay?

With that, Mari relaxed back against the soft feather pillows of the big four-poster bed and nodded her understanding. Big tears slid down the sides of her face to land in her ears. She was so ashamed and filled with loss. The gift that she wanted to give John had been stolen.

Nelly rallied her staff, and soon a hot saltwater bath awaited a very stiff and sore Mari. Nelly and Bella, Billy's mom, helped Mari out of her night rail and had to stifle their gasps when they saw all her deep bruises. Mari stepped into the large copper tub and sunk down into its welcome warmth. She sighed as the pain soaked from her body. Nelly washed her hair, using some lavender soap she had and dried her off with a thick soft towel. Bella brought her a clean night rail, wrapper, and slippers. After she was dressed, Billy brought her up something to eat. It was just some broth and soft bread which she dunked into the broth and ate gingerly.

John also awoke in a panic, as wave after wave of pain washed over him. He tried to sit up, but Wills pushed him gently back down.

"Wow, son. Relax now. Everything will be alright, but you have to stay still John. Those bastards busted you up real bad."

John placed a hand over his ribs and looked up at Dr. Wills with pain-glazed eyes before breathlessly gasping, "Mari. They, they hurt her."

Dr. Wills patted Johns hand and stated with tenderness, "Yes, John, they did. But you… Lord only knows how… stopped them from completing the deed."

"Dr. Wills, where, where is she?"

"Here, John!" Mari yelled as she ran into the room. Thunder attempted to smile, but found that it too brought him pain. Raising his hand slowly, he motioned for her to come and sit beside him on the bed. She looked to the others for approval, and when they nodded that it was okay, she gingerly curled up beside him, placing her hand in his. With great effort, and ignoring the pain, he slowly brought her hand to his cut and swollen lips. She held her breath as he brushed a kiss upon her palm and whispered, *"Ne'me'hota'tsa meoon."*

Dr. Wills and Nelly looked over at her, puzzled, and Wills asked, "What did he say?"

With tears running down her very relieved cheeks, she said, "He said, 'I love you sweetheart'."

Nelly dashed the tears from her own eyes and said as she left the room. "I'll go and fetch em some broth too"

"And a pot for some tea too Ms. Nelly," Dr. Wills piped in.

"Willow bark tea mixed with chamomile," Mari chimed in. "It will relax his muscles and help with the pain." When she saw how they looked at her, she said, "John's been teaching me. Besides, I could use some too." She smiled sheepishly. "I take mine with honey."

When Nelly came back with the tray, Mari got up gingerly and went to make the tea from Thunder's herbs. While she was in the other room, Thunder Heart asked Dr. Wills about their injuries. Wills pulled no punches. He explained completely what the brutes had done to Mari, and though she was traumatized, he felt she would heal with no ill effects. He also told John that he had several broken ribs, a broken nose, a fractured jaw severe bruising to his internal organs and a sutured laceration that covered a knot the size of a goose egg on the back of his head. Attempting to smile he said, "Thanks, Dr. Wills, for telling me. I thought it would be worse." Dr. Wills bristled a little, but seeing the twinkle in John's eyes, he gave way to a good-hearted laugh.

Mari giggled too, saying, "The Indians say laughter is good medicine."

"That it is Lass," Dr. Wills stated. "But don't be tickling his fancy for a while yet. Understand? He has a lot of healing to do. I don't want him laughing for quite a while."

"Trust me, sir. I'll behave, and so will he. I'll make sure of it." Her eyes twinkled with a glee she could hardly contain.

CHAPTER 26: HEALING

While the initial shock of the incident resolved itself quickly, their complete healing would take a lot more time, however. While Mari's physical injuries healed rapidly, she still suffered nightmares and no one said a thing when they found her curled up in bed beside John.

John's injuries didn't heal as quickly, and when Dr. Wills had to return to the hospital, Mr. Lee and his son came to help. The healing herbs, teas, and poultices that they brought were very effective in his recovery.

Mari stayed by Thunder Heart's side, day and night, as he drifted in and out of consciousness. After five days, Thunder Heart awakened fully and the first thing he saw was Mari's sweet face. Even covered with discolored bruises, she was a beautiful sight to him. He winced as he took a deep breath and she quickly awakened.

"Oh, thank God you're back," she said. "I was so afraid I would loose you, too."

He stroked her cheek gently and stated, "No, *meoon*, I will never leave you. I will always be at your side. I'm so sorry you were hurt. I put you in danger by keeping you so near."

"No, John. It was my fault. I should never have kissed you in public. You told me that people would not approve of our love, but somehow, being so in love with you, I couldn't believe it would be so bad that people would try to kill you. I'm so very sorry my love."

"You still wish to be my wife, Mari?"

"More than ever, John. No small-minded bastards are going to make me stop loving you... but do you still want me?" She dropped her eyes and whispered, "I'm not a virgin anymore."

Reaching up, he cupped her cheek in his hand and caressed her bruise with his thumb. "*Ma'heo'o* chose well for me. He blessed me beyond measure when I found you, and you will be my wife and I will be the first man to make love to you."

Brushing the hair from his face she leaned over him and kissed him gently. "Rest now, my love, and heal quickly. We have a honeymoon to get ready for."

Seeing all the love that radiated toward him from her eyes, he smiled and whispered, "I can hardly wait, *mitawin.*"

"John, why do you keep calling me 'wife'?"

Thunder looked deeply into her eyes and stated, as he ran his thumb over her bottom lip, "My sweet, sweet Mari, it's because in my heart you are already my wife."

"Oh, John, I feel the same. I don't know if you've noticed, but I have been sleeping with you. I tried sleeping in my room but I have such nightmares and they only go away when I am resting with you."

Thunder took a deep breath and replied, "I knew you were beside me and I am truly sorry about your nightmares, but to tell you the truth, having you near helped me rest better, also. When I would wake up in fear for you, I would see your sweet face and my anxiety would go away. Now woman, this man is hungry. Could you see if Ms. Nelly has some stew for me?"

Mari scurried off the bed pulled on her day dress and hurried down the stairs.

After three weeks, Thunder Heart was getting restless, and though he still felt some pain in his ribs, he returned to work with Mari at his side. Now, he carried his knife and used a four-foot walking stick to aid his steps. Mr. Lee had given it to him, stating that this stick in the hands of a true warrior was as good as any two-by-four. Thunder Heart smiled when he thought of it. He liked Mr. Lee. He reminded him of his great uncle Quiet Waters.

And so things went along well for John and Mari. Most of the people that John had helped had returned home, but he had made many lasting friends. Dr. Wills enjoyed teaching Thunder Heart and his skills in surgery were remarkable. He wished he could offer him a permanent place at the hospital, but sadly this could not be. Maybe someday when people weren't so prejudiced, a doctor would be judged by his skill and not by the color of his skin.

After two more weeks, John and Mari's bruises had all but faded away, and Dr. Wills asked them again to attend a formal dinner at his home the following day. They agreed, and since it had been a short day at the hospital, they went shopping.

Before they entered the mercantile, they were warmly greeted by a smiling Sergeant O'Malley.

"Thunder, me boy, tis a pleasure to be seein' ye today." He tipped his hat at Mari and slapped Thunder on the back. "I wanted to tell ye that the head office has approved me retirement. What do you think, me boy,

if I went and settled in Dream Valley? Do ye think yer people would let me?"

Thunder smiled broadly as he pumped his old friend's hand. "Uncle, I know my people would be most honored to have you settle there. When are you planning your journey?"

"Well, I'm not sure as yet. I have to see if the store keep has gotten in me order, and if he has, then, well, I thought I would be leaving very soon. I have such plans for the valley and I hope your people will help me turn it into a real fine little farm town."

"Well, Uncle, they will be pleased. I know that you have a lot to teach my people and it would be most beneficial for them if they could become more self sufficient. The white world holds to much danger for them. Our people need to remain separate, at least until society becomes more tolerant. Oh, and Uncle, not to change the subject, but Mari and I are going to have a dinner at Dr. Wills' home tomorrow. We would love to have you there. Could you come, say, around one pm?"

"It would be my pleasure, me boy," he replied, slapping Thunder on the shoulder. "Now, let us go in here and conduct our business."

Mari took Thunder's arm and the three went inside. Mari loved the store. It reminded her of her father's store back home. Shelves stacked from floor to ceiling with everything imaginable, and the smells, oh the smells, were so wonderful. Dill from the pickle barrels, lavender and rose from the ladies' soaps, leather tanned to perfection, and cedar along with fresh milled oak. Mari took a deep breath, closing her eyes briefly and savored the memories the store invoked.

The store keeper was glad to see them, and when Thunder and Mari explained what they were looking for, he quickly showed them his finest formal wear, while the sergeant checked over his order in the back room. John tried on several suits before choosing a conservative dark blue one with a black vest, white shirt, and a black string tie. Mari chose a pale blue satin gown with a low neckline and a wide lace collar. When they brought their choices to the front desk, they found that the store keeper had added a gold pocket watch and a pair of white satin slippers to their order. John frowned, but the store keeper smiled and said that they were gifts to them from him because of all the business they had given him.

John paid the man and shook his hand firmly. "Sir," John stated. "It is I who must thank you for your kindness. You risked a lot to service me, and you have not once looked down on my Indian blood or disrespected Mari for being with me. I thank you, and promise to give you a lot more of my business before I return to my people."

The store keeper stood up proudly, and taking Thunder's hand again, smiled as he firmly shook it. "It has been a privilege, Dr. Heart, a real privilege."

They gathered their packages then, got into their carriage and left for the Hotel.

When Bella saw Mari and John pull up outside, she called Billy to help with the packages before he returned the carriage back to the livery.

"Ms. Nelly has dinner ready in the dinning room," called Bella. "You might as well come and eat it before it gets cold."

"Thank you, Bella," Mari stated as they entered the beautifully-decorated dining room. "I guess you noticed we went shopping." She giggled as John helped her take her seat. "Dr. Wills has invited us to a formal dinner at his home tomorrow. Isn't that grand?"

"Why, yes, it is," stated Nelly. "Did you find a nice dress, Mari?"

"Oh, I did indeed. It is a pale blue and it's the most beautiful dress I have ever seen, let alone owned. You will have to come up after dinner and see it. The store owner even gave me a pair of satin slippers to wear with it."

Mari was so happy and bubbly. John couldn't help but smile. He loved seeing her this way, and when he noticed the knowing glances Nelly and Bella gave each other, he suddenly realized that the women had been planning the same thing he and Dr. Wills had. Sipping his coffee quietly, smiling to himself, he let her go on and on about her new dress, knowing full well that tomorrow it would be her wedding gown.

Later that night he brewed up a relaxing tea for them both. He knew that neither of them would get any sleep if he didn't. The sexual tension that was building between them was almost more than he could stand. He found excuses to avoid her all that afternoon and evening, but when they went to bed, he pulled her gently into his arms. She was so relaxed and he reveled in the sensual feel of her body. He ran his fingers through her soft curls and kissed her deeply as he caressed her soft folds. He made love to her with his hands and lips until she shuddered in wave after wave of pleasure. When she had fallen into a blissful sleep he got up and went to the privy to lessen his need, but it only took the edge off. Tomorrow he would make her fully his.

CHAPTER 27: JOY

The next morning, John got up before Mari to find that the house was already bustling with activity. He ate a hurried breakfast and retrieved his suit from Bella, who had pressed it for him. Draping the suit over his arm he left for the stable out back. Passing Ms. Nelly he stated, "Nelly, please tell Mari that I had to go see some patients and that if I am not back by noon, that she is to dress and meet me at the doctor's home, okay?"

Nelly giggled and said she would handle it, and would make sure she got there on time. "Now off with ya now and don'y ya be a wrinklin' that suit or getting it smellin' of horse leather. Ya hear me?"

"I hear you, Nelly," he said over his shoulder as he rode off.

Mari came down the back stairs slowly around eight thirty am. She had never slept in for so long. She had donned a plaid day dress and brushed and quickly pinned her long hair up off her neck. When she reached the dining room, she looked around for Thunder, and when she didn't find him, she went to the kitchen.

"Nelly, where is John? And if you don't mind me asking, why are you cooking so much food today?"

"Well, child, Dr. John was called out to meet Dr. Wills and Dr. Wills said he had to move the dinner up to three pm. So he wants you there at one pm."

Nelly could see the puzzlement on Mari's face, and held up her hand. "Now, I know plans got changed, but Bella is goin' to help ya get ready, and I am preparin' some extra food for the dinner."

"Oh, Nelly, I'm so happy. John will be so surprised won't he?"

"Yes, he will, child, since he is expectin' you to wear that blue dress, and you're not."

"What do you mean I'm not?"

Bella came out then giggling. "No, you're not," she said. "If you go to your closet again you'll find something special there for you."

Mari's heart beat wildly as she raced up the back stairs to her room. Her hands shook as she opened the closet door and her eyes instantly filled with tears as she beheld the most beautiful wedding gown she had ever seen. Gingerly, she took it out of the closet and held it up before her. She couldn't believe her eyes as she looked at herself in the floor length mirror that stood regally in the corner of her room. It was like a fairy tale dream. Bella came in as she was laying it gently across the bed.

Turning toward her friend, Mari asked, "Oh Bella where did it come from?"

"Nelly and I made it," Bella stated. "Do you like it?"

Mari couldn't control the tears that began to fall, and gladly accepted a sisterly hug. Bella patted her back and dried her tears on the corner of her apron before stating, "Now, now, Mari, you don't have time for tears, lass. We have to get started getting you ready if we are to have you at the good doctor's house by noon."

Mari nodded and went straight to the tub that awaited her.

She languished in the hot bubbles that smelled strongly of lavender, and she was so relaxed that Bella had to come in and hurry her out. Bella helped her dress in her blue gown and fixed her hair. Mari thought she had never looked so beautiful and wished her brother could have been here to see her.

Hurrying down the stairs, the two women headed to the awaiting carriage. Nelly's husband helped her get aboard. Then he helped Bella get in, being careful not to touch the white gown and veil she carried.

When they arrived at Dr. Wills' house, the women hurried inside and up the front stairs where they would remain until the good doctor came for them.

Mari did not see any of the preparations that were going on down stairs, and by the time John arrived with Dr. Wills from the hospital, all the preparations were done and the guests had arrived. John went into the doctor's library and quickly changed into his suit.

Dr. Wills had a huge home, and the women and servants had

opened up the doors between the two parlors and the dinning room. The tables were pushed back next to the walls and decorated with flowers and candles. Since they didn't have enough chairs for all the guests, it was standing room only on either side of the long red floor runner. When Thunder came out of the library, he almost panicked at the sight of the white man's opulent splendor, but relaxed when he saw all the guests were people he knew, such as: Mr. Lee and his family, Nelly and her husband along with Billy Blue Hawk. There was Mr. Jones, the store owner, Mr. Olson from the livery, Ed the blacksmith, Sam from the Saloon, Mr. Wong Lee, and all the patients John had helped, including a few of the soiled doves. He walked down the aisle and stood nervously, waiting next to Pastor Johnson and Sergeant O'Malley who he had been secretly asked to be his best man.

When Dr. Wills went upstairs for Mari, she was more than ready and on the verge of panic. Her heart was beating so fast, and she was restlessly pacing. Bella had changed into Mari's blue gown and would act as her maid of honor.

Dr. Wills, noticing her anxious state, walked over to her and took hold of one of her hands and kissed it.

"Mari, my child, you are breathtaking," Dr. Wills said with a smile. "Except there is something missing."

"Oh my," Mari gasped. "What is it? I thought I remembered everything."

"No, no my dear," he said. "I have it right here." Dr. Wills reached into his vest pocket and pulled out a strand of pearls and placed them around her neck. "Now we have everything."

Mari's eyes misted over as she touched them gingerly. "Oh, Dr. Wills, they're beautiful. Thank you oh so very much for everything."

"It's my pleasure child. Now, no more dawdling, we need to go now."

Dr. Wills took her arm then, tucking it through his, and led the ladies toward the stairs. Bella, carrying the flowers, which consisted of red roses and white prairie flowers, headed down the marble staircase first to the sound of the pastor's wife playing the wedding march on the piano.

John's heart started racing as he saw the hem of Mari's blue dress coming down the stairs, but was completely taken aback when he saw that it was Bella wearing the dress. Then filled with anticipation anew, he was awestruck as Dr. Wills and a shimmering white satin gown descended the stairs. Finally he could see his Mari. She looked like an angel clothed in moon beams, and once their eyes met, they saw nothing and no one else. When she reached him Dr. Wills nodded to John and went to sit down. John lifted her veil and trailed his fingertips down her cheek, causing a shiver of pleasure to cascade down her spine. Then he took her trembling hands in his and softly caressed their backs with his thumbs as he spoke to her in Cheyenne. Later, when they were alone, he would tell her what he had said. When he was through vowing his undying love to her, the pastor began the service.

When he got to the part where he asked them to repeat after him, Mari was very surprised to hear Pastor Johnson use John's full name, but relaxed when John lifted his chin proudly and lovingly repeated the old pledge to love, honor and cherish her till death do they part. And when it was her turn, to show him the sincerity of her pledge to love honor and obey, she stood tall, also with her chin up. And even though her eyes were glistening with tears of joy, she repeated the words without hesitation. Then before they knew it, they were pronounced husband and wife and it was time to kiss the bride.

John, smiling broadly, his eyes glistening with joy, took her face between his large, strong hands and kissed her so lovingly that tears filled the eyes of their guests. It was then that the cameraman Dr. Wills hired snapped a picture, filling the room with the acid smell of flash powder and broke the magical moment, thus triggering a cacophony of loud shouts to erupt from the guests and they were bombarded with hugs, handshakes, and back slaps.

The meal that followed was wonderful, and there were servants passing trays of food and drinks all around, even out to the people that sat on the lawn. Everyone who came talked, laughed and generally had a good time. After the meal was finished, John and Mari cut their cake and then set about meeting each and every guest. Many of the guests in the house were white, and the gifts they brought were left inside Dr. Wills' study to be unwrapped later, but the people that were outside meant more to Thunder Heart and Mari. These were the poor, the Indians, the Chinese, and the soiled doves that John and Mari had taken care of. They had watched the service but went outside afterward because they felt uncomfortable mixing with white society, or rather, society was uncomfortable mixing with them.

An elderly Indian couple met them as they crossed the lawn and presented them with a mule that John accepted with a great show of pride, and Mari shed tears openly when a young Indian couple came forward with their baby. This, Mari realized, was John's miracle baby. John lovingly took the child into his arms and placed a kiss on the boy's soft head, and the mother handed Mari a beautiful hand-beaded pair of baby moccasins and spoke to her in her native tongue.

John translated for her. "Mari. This is Gentle Touch and her husband Works Hard. They want to thank us for their child and her life. She made these shoes for our baby."

"Tell them thank you, John, and that the shoes are beautiful and our child will wear them with pride, and that their son is greatly blessed to have such wonderful parents."

John said just that, and he also told the couple that they would always be welcomed with much respect in their home and in his village over the mountain if ever they came that way. John shook the young man's hand and handed him back the baby, and Mari hugged the young mother. Everyone who saw this swelled with pride for this couple who looked so white, but who acted so kindly toward everyone, accepting the humble gifts as if they were worth a fortune. But what the wealthy didn't realize was that those gifts given out of love and sacrifice were priceless to John and Mari. Things such as: a cooking pot, a bag of teas, a feather fan, a hand crocheted shawl, a hand carved cradle board, a bow, a beaded quiver, a pie, some soap scented with lavender and rose petals, and even a wrapped box from the doves that they were not to open until they were home alone.

As the sun began to set, music filled the air, and people started dancing. Mari waltzed with every man there, but most often found herself within her husband's loving arms, and as they waltzed around the parlor, all they could think about was being back in their room at the hotel making love.

Once Mari had waltzed around the parlor for what felt to her like one hundred times, she grabbed John's hand and pleaded: "John darling, PLEASE let's go. I can't dance another step."

John, being sick of watching every man in the room holding his woman, was all too happy to comply. After making the announcement that they were leaving, Mari tossed her bouquet, which was caught by one of the doves, and they were pelted with handfuls of rice as they fled rapidly hand-in-hand out the front door to the awaiting carriage.

Once they were on their way, John pulled Mari into his arms, and as he ran his fingers up her neck, he brushed his lips over hers and felt her tremble. Passionately he ran his tongue over her lips, and as shivers of pleasure flooded her body, she opened her lips for him and he deepened the kiss. They were still kissing when the carriage arrived at Nelly's, and Mari blushed and giggled as the driver loudly cleared his throat.

"A-hummmm!"

John got down from the carriage, reached into his suit pocket, and handed the driver some cash as he shook his hand, thanking him for his service. The driver looking quickly at the bill and was shocked to find it to be a fifty dollar note. He had just made three month's wages in one day and gladly stated, "Thank ye, sir."

"It is I who thank you, sir, for seeing us safely to our door," John stated with a smile as he scooped Mari into his arms. He carried his giggling, trembling prize all the way up the walk, through the large double doors, and right up the stairs to their rooms, which had been transformed into a flower-filled bridal suite.

Thunder sat her down gently, turning her back to him. She stood there, quivering with anticipation, as he took the ribbon from her hair and quickly shrugged out of his jacket and shirt, tossing them onto the bedside chair. Then he started unbuttoning her dress, trailing kisses down her neck as he went, sending shivers down her spine and heat pooling low in her belly. Soon, the dress slid down her slender form to pool at her feet on the floor, which she stepped out of. He pulled her back into him, and as she rested her tiny body against the hard length of him, he wrapped his arms around her to caress her breasts through her chemise.

Letting out a moan of pleasure, Mari reached up and pulled the blue ribbon that held her slip and it fell from her body as well.

She turned around within his arms and she heard him gasp as her hardened nipples brushed his bare chest. She reached up and took his face within her tiny hands and pulled him to her awaiting lips. Taking her into his arms, he kissed her with all the love he possessed. Then, lifting her like a child in his arms, he carried her to the awaiting feather bed. Laying her gently upon the crisp white sheets, he broke the kiss just long enough to kick off his boots and pants before joining her there. Mari also took that time to divest herself of her remaining clothing, and now lay resplendently naked before him. As he gazed upon her luscious form, she looked fully upon him for the first time. She wasn't afraid of his fully aroused state, but rather found his body beautiful and exciting. All she knew was that he was her husband and she wanted him. She reached out, and he entered her arms, quickly molding his strong hard body to hers.

John kissed and caressed every part of her, driving her passion higher and higher until she cried out in pleasure, then he positioned himself between her thighs, his erection meeting her opening. He looked into her passion-glazed eyes and began to slowly and gently enter her, but she didn't stiffen when he felt her body's tight resistance, she just smiled and said, "John, do it, do it now. Make me fully yours. I need to feel you within me. Make us one."

John took hold of her bottom then, and pulled her to him as he thrust forward. She cried out once and he kissed her deeply and held her to him until she relaxed within his arms. She felt so good, he thought. His Mari, his woman, so soft and warm and wet. He had dreamed of this moment for so long, and he marveled at how her body had stretched to accommodate his size so well. He kissed her again, stroking her breasts, taking her to new heights of passion as he started to slowly thrust within her, but before long, her heated passion matched his own and she tipped her pelvis and met him with thrusts of her own. Suddenly, as heaven washed over her again, she felt him stiffen and groan as he poured his life within her. It was heaven, she thought, and as he slumped over her, spent, his body glistening with perspiration, she held his weight and brushed his moist hair from his handsome face. As she held his resting head to her breast, she realized that no mater where her man lived, it would be home to her. She said, "*Na'me'hota'tsa*, my husband."

After he had caught his breath, he rolled them to their sides, still remaining united as one flesh. He caressed her face, placing kisses over her cheeks and on her eyes and let the tears of his profound joy slide down his cheeks.

"Oh, Mari, my love," he said. "I feel so complete in your arms. It's like I have finally come home. I thought I would never love any woman again after I lost Dancing Moon, but then I found an angel lying on a beach. Even ice cold and blue, you stole my heart from me. I tried to run from it. Fought hard to deny it, but in the end, I realized I had come to love you and had to make you mine. Today, I thought I could never love you more than I already did but I have to tell you, that now after making you truly mine, I love you so much more right now that I don't have the words to even express it."

She smiled sweetly and stated while caressing the tears from his face,

"You don't have to say anything, John. Just show me."

He did just that again and again, all night long.

CHAPTER 28: LOSS AND ANGER

One evening, about a week after the wedding, John came home from work towing an old mare behind his horse. When he headed behind the hotel to the small barn, Billy met him there.

"Wow, Dr. John, sir, where did you get her?"

Thunder heart got down from his horse and handed Billy the reigns to the mare, then he replied, "Billy, she was given to me in payment for services, but I am giving her to you. She needs some good looking after and I know you will treat her well, and besides I thought you could bring me messages faster if you had your own mount."

Billy didn't know what to say as his eyes filled with tears. Suddenly, he grabbed John around the waist and hugged him fiercely.

"I'll take good care of her, sir. You'll see. You'll get your messages real fast from now on."

"I know I will Billy, but remember she's an old horse and you shouldn't run her too fast for too long".

"Yes, sir, Dr. John. I'll remember and I'll take such good care of her. You'll hardly recognize her when I'm done." He hurriedly took both horses into the barn.

After several hours, Billy came running into the house and seeing the women in the kitchen, he excitedly called, "Mom, Nelly, Mari come out and see the horse Dr. John just gave me. Come on, hurry, you gots to see. I gots her all cleaned up and she's so beautiful."

The women and John followed the boy to the barn, and John was so pleased with what he saw. The boy had bathed the old horse and brushed her coat until it shone. He even polished her hooves.

"Oh Billy," his mother cried. "She is a beautiful thing. But John, you shouldn't have."

Before Billy could react with disappointment, John replied as he laid his hand on the boy's shoulder.

"Bella, your son will be a man soon, and a man needs his own mount. I know that his father would have already given him one by now. I don't mean to be presumptuous, Bella, but I feel the boy has earned it for all the running he has done for me."

Bella went to hug her son, and while she petted the horse, she told John thank you. Then patting Billy's back, she said, "You did a good job on her, son. Put her to bed now and come in and wash up. It's time for supper."

She fished an apple out of her apron pocket she'd been saving for an evening snack, and gave it to the horse before stating to her son, "If you take good care of her, she'll take care of you. That's what your pa would say. And besides, she looks like she needed a friend."

"Yeah, Ma, next to Dr. John, she's my best friend. I'm gonna call her Star cause of the Star on her forehead."

Everyone agreed it was a good name for the mare, and they all realized right then that they had never seen Billy look so happy. That evening as they ate their supper of chicken and dumplings and apple pie, everyone felt very blessed.

By mid-July, Thunder Heart had received the results of his exam and found he had passed it with very high marks and Mari was fast becoming his skilled nurse.

He could have quickly built a large practice within the lower classes of Vancouver, but he longed to return home, and once there, he and Mari would marry again in the tradition of his ancestors. So in the month of tall grass, they made their plans to return to Mist Valley where he would set up his practice.

On the night before their scheduled departure, there came a loud pounding on their door. Thunder threw a blanket around his naked form and hurriedly answered it to find Billy looking wild-eyed and as frightened as a kid could get.

"Billy, what's wrong?" Thunder asked as he laid a reassuring hand on the trembling boys shoulder.

"It's – it's my ma, sir. You gots to come quick, she's bleedin' real bad."

"Okay Billy, where is she?"

"Downstairs in our room by the kitchen."

"Okay Billy, I'll be right there," he said as he jerked on his pants and moccasins. Waking Mari with a firm shake he asked for her to follow him down with some clean towels. He grabbed his black leather bag and flew down the stairs with Billy speaking rapid fire.

"Ma, she started feelin' poorly last week. Upchucking and all. Then today she started having stomach cramps and she went to bed early. Now she's in a lot a pain, sir, and she's bleedin' somethin' fierce."

When Thunder got to the room, he found Bella lying on the floor in a pool of blood. He scooped her up and laid her on the bed and told Billy to go get Mari and Ms. Nelly quickly.

As John examined her, he found that she had miscarried and was hemorrhaging.

"Bella, Bella what happened?" he asked as he shook her more fully awake.

She weakly replied, "I went to see old lady Jade. I got pregnant and I couldn't support it, so I paid her to get rid of it for me."

"Oh, Bella," he said with such anguish. "I wish you would have come to me instead. You have lost a lot of blood and I fear I will have to operate to save you but that still may not be possible."

She took his hand and asked him to take care of Billy if she should die. John smiled and placing a kiss on her fevered brow said, "I will be honored to have Billy for a son. I promise I will teach him everything he needs to know to become a good man, and I will send him to school also."

"Thank you, John. You're a good man."

Mari, Ms. Nelly and Billy returned just then, and he told Billy to sit up at his mom's head and keep talking to her while he and Mari set about performing a vaginal hysterectomy to stop the bleeding and try to save her life.

Thunder Heart worked feverishly, but the blood literally poured from her body. "The old hag Jade must have punctured her uterine artery," he stated as he grabbed a handful of gauze to stuff up inside her vaginal opening.

"My GOD Mari!" he cried. "Push down on her stomach, hard! I

can't stop the bleeding!"

Mari pushed down with all her might, but John sadly shook his head. He packed her vaginal canal tightly with gauze, washed up, then covered her, and opened the bedroom door. Wiping his hands dry, he said to Billy, "Talk to her son, there isn't much time."

Everyone stepped out of the room then to allow the boy to spend his last minutes with his beloved mother alone.

Mari, with tears streaming down her face, flung herself into John's arms.

"Oh, John, it's so sad and so unfair. She was so good and worked so hard. What will Billy do now?"

"I told Bella I would take Billy as my son," he said. "And this I will do. I will see that he has a good education and is trained in the ways of a man of the people. Then he will be able to decide what path he will take when he is grown."

Mari smiled up at him and softly caressed his worry-wrinkled face. "I love you, John."

"And I love you too, *mitawin*. We will leave this place the day after tomorrow, taking Billy with us. I can no longer bear to live in the white man's world any longer. But for today I must go see a certain Ms. Jade and confront her on what she has done."

Mari had never seen her husband so angry. The fire in his eyes frightened her, and she feared for his safety. Wrapping her arms around him, she thought to hold him until he calmed down, but she knew by his ridged posture that she couldn't hold him.

"I'll go with you," Mari stated firmly.

"NO!" Thunder snapped, the anger he felt barely suppressed. "You are needed here. Help get her ready for burial when her spirit has finally fled. I will be back soon. I promise."

Thunder grabbed up a towel, wiped off as much blood as possible from his clothes, and stormed out the front door. He paid no attention to the gasps of fright his bloody clothes elicited as he walked down the street. His heart was filled with hatred— hatred at the ignorance and injustice that would lead someone to do such a horrible thing to another human being.

Billy came out of the room not long after John left and Mari enfolded the lad within her trembling arms. The boy broke down and wept then. "She was such a good momma. She always worked so hard and never complained, even when Pa drank and beat her. She was so happy when she met that Mr. Anderson. She told me he had asked her to marry him. I knew it was too good to be true when I saw him leave by boat last week. He did this to her didn't he, Miss Mari?"

"Oh Billy," she said as she walked the boy over to sit on the settee in the hall. "Do you know why she died?"

"Yeah, she had Old Lady Jade kill the baby she carried and it killed her too. Why did she do that? Havin' a babe ain't bad, is it?"

"Well, Billy, it is for an unmarried woman. Without a man to help and protect her, people would have treated her like a whore and the child would have been treated even worse than they treat you. She was desperate Billy, and desperate people do desperate things. She wanted better for herself and for you."

Billy sat there with Mari on the settee just outside Bella's room. Mari hugged him tightly to her as he cried his heart out.

Thunder Heart charged into the livery and retrieved his other horse. He didn't waste time saddling the steed. He just leaped onto its back and rode hard toward the side of town that the people called China Town. He stopped and dismounted his horse in front of a saloon called the Red Pagoda. Everyone in town knew this was a house of prostitution and if he meant to find Old Lady Jade, and he did, here was where to look. He stormed into the lobby and was met by a sweet, shy celestial.

"How can we serve you, Dr. John, sir?" she asked as she bowed low before him.

His eyes met hers and he felt such pity for her. He hated this kind of life that some women were forced to live, but he didn't come here to rescue damsels in distress. He wanted Lady Jade.

With his eyes hard with anger he stated firmly through gritted teeth, "Where can I find Lady Jade?"

"Lady Jade? Why do you seek her, doctor?"

Thunder knew he needed to calm his temper especially here. There were guards every where and he didn't relish another beating so he thought fast and replied,

"I need to talk to her about her medicine?"

"Oh, yes, doctor. I will go ask if she will speak to you."

She left him standing while she went down a long hall to a room in the back of the house. John noted how the house was decorated in red silk and watercolor paintings of China and other scenes that helped keep the place looking calm and relaxing for the men that waited their turns with the ladies who worked there.

The young lady returned quickly and bowed again saying, "The Lady Jade will see you now."

He followed her down the hall to the last room on the left. She knocked and when she heard a frail voice call out, she opened the door and Thunder entered. The room was bright and some areas were separated from others by paper screens. The air was heavy with incense and the sound of glass chimes filled the air. John found Jade sitting in a fan back chair in front of a window overlooking a small but beautiful garden. Meeting John's hard gaze with one of her own, she noticed the blood on his clothes, but did not show any emotion except curiosity.

"What can I do for you, Dr. Heart?" she said.

John came over to her and sat in a chair across from her, placing his clasped hands on the table before him.

He took a deep, calming breath and let it out slowly before stating through clenched teeth, "Lady Jade, Mrs. Blue Hawk is dead. She bled to death."

The woman looked disinterested while she puffed on her small pipe.

"I am here, Ms. Jade, to teach you how to keep more women you help alive."

Jade smiled and asked, "Why do you think I need your teaching?"

"While you think you are a very wise woman, Jade, your patients suffer from infections and severe bleeding. I know that I can not stop women from seeking your help, and I do not wish to do so if it is their wish, but you must use proper precautions and use special herbal teas afterward to prevent bleeding. Would you be willing to do this?"

"Dr. John, you are a very rare man. I can see in your eyes you would like to kill me, but instead, you offer teaching. I am not a cruel woman. I only seek to help those women that are suffering from cruel, lying men and those poor doves who have been caught by nature, and no man will marry them. So, yes, Dr. Heart, teach me how to do what I do better."

It didn't take long for him to outline the procedures to prevent infection and show her the teas to use to cure the effects of the abortion and help to heal the women. He told Jade that he would have Mr. Wong Lee to send her over the teas she would need. She thanked him and stated her regrets at the loss of Mrs. Blue Hawk. Thunder nodded then and departed, feeling the anger draining from him only to be replaced with sadness because he had to stop by the undertakers and make arrangements for yet another burial.

Once done Thunder rode back to the hotel with a very heavy heart.

Mari greeted him with a hug as he entered the hotel. His heart wept for the boy even as his arms enfolded around his sweetheart, and Mari could feel his trembling sorrow.

"How is the boy?" he asked.

She replied, "I gave him some of your calming tea and he is asleep in our spare room."

"Good, *mitawin*. Are you packed and ready for our trip?"

"Yes, John, all except for Billy's things. I don't know which of his mother's things he wishes to keep."

"She has very little Mari," he stated. "So after the undertaker takes her, we will go through the room looking through every hiding place and pack all of her personal things up for Billy to take with him. While you do that, sweetheart, I will go to the mercantile and buy him and you some warm boots and coats for the journey. It will take us over a week of hard traveling to get there and the temperature is cold in the mountains."

Hugging him tight to her again, she smiled weakly and said, "John, while Billy is resting, why don't we both get some rest? You look so very tired."

"Yes Mari, I am, but I wish only to hold you for a while."

They walked back up the stairs to their room. Thunder removed his soiled clothing and Mari curled up next to him on the bed. Finally she felt his trembling cease and they drifted off to sleep. Once asleep and dreaming, Thunder Heart found himself standing in Mist Valley. He could hear the thunder of pounding hooves becoming louder and louder as they headed in his direction, but he didn't move. Suddenly the thundering stopped, and the mist parted. He found himself once again face to face with the White Buffalo.

"Son of Quiet Hawk," Wakan Tonka said. "I am pleased to find that your heart still thunders for your people and you are returning home, but you must prepare to fight a great battle. A great sickness comes to the people. One only you can fight. Prepare and travel quickly for it has already begun."

Before Thunder Heart could reply, he awakened, and not wanting to awaken Mari, he tried to hold very still as he took deep slow breaths to calm his nerves. As he lay there staring up at the cracked plaster on the ceiling, he went over and over the words of his totem in his mind.

There was a great sickness back home he had to fight. He would see Mr. Lee and prepare to face any number of white man's illnesses. He just prayed he would make it home in time. The good part was that he hadn't seen his father's hawk yet.

CHAPTER 30: THE JOURNEY HOME

They buried Billy's mother next to Mari's brother later that evening and Thunder Heart sang for her soul. He hugged Billy close to his side. Billy was his son now, and he would make sure he had everything his poor mother had wanted him to have: love, an education, and a chance to grow up to be an honorable man. While the gravediggers filled in the grave, Thunder spoke to the boy.

"Billy, did I tell you I have a son around your age? His name is Winter Blue. I think he will be happy to have a brother. His mother died at his birth, and he is being raised by my sister. I have missed him very much and can't wait to see him again."

"Sir, what do you mean?" Billy hopefully asked. "Does this mean you are taking me with you? To your village to be your son?"

Patting Billy's shoulder, Thunder Heart gazed deeply into the child's grieving eyes. "Yes Billy, I am. Before your mother passed, she asked me to look after you. Now, come on, let's leave here. Your mother is at peace now. Her spirit lives on in you, son. As long as you are alive she will always be with you."

"I know Sir," Billy said. "And I will make you and her proud of me. I'm really lookin' forward to meetin' your family and ta going ta school. I will get ta go to school won't I, sir?"

"Yes Billy, that's a promise. Every boy and girl in my village has to go to school."

Placing a comforting hand on the boy's shoulder, Thunder took Mari's hand and they left the cemetery.

Before they returned to the hotel though, they stopped by the general store to make their purchases for their journey to Mist Valley. The store keeper told John that he would have everything packed and loaded on mules and delivered to the Hotel in the morning. John thanked the man for everything he had done for him and the store keeper thanked John for his business and bid them all a safe trip.

After that they stopped by Mr. Wong Lee's so he could purchase some large quantities of the herbs he couldn't find in the mountains. Mr. Wong Lee had anticipated John's eventual return home and had ordered extra herbs, all too happy to provide Thunder with everything he required. After another sad farewell, they finally returned to the hotel.

As they were getting down from the carriage in front of the hotel, they were met by Sergeant O'Malley. The sergeant held out his hand and Thunder took it. "I am sorry I haven't been around lately, me boy, but the Queen and Country had one last mission for me to complete."

John looked at his friend quizzically. "One last mission. Does this mean you are free from your job now, Uncle Will?" he asked.

Sergeant O'Malley slapped Thunder on the back and laughingly stated, "Oh yes, me boy. I am now a free man. I heard that you were leavin' tomorrow for home and I was wonderin' if I could travel with ya? I have plans to build a gristmill and sawmill in Dream Valley. Do you think the council will approve?"

John beamed. "I think that's a wonderful idea. We leave at sun up tomorrow. Will you be ready to leave by then?"

"I'm already packed, loaded and ready to go. I'll see ya in the mornin' lad." He tipped his hat at Mari and stated, "Evenin' Mamma."

Then he mounted his horse and rode away.

The sun rose bright and hot the next morning as they prepared to head out. Dr. Wills and Ms. Nelly stood on the hotel front porch, watching the young couple readying their belongings to depart. Nelly's eyes were misty and she kept dabbing at them with the corner of her apron. She wanted so badly for them to stay, but after what they had already been through at the hands of small-minded people, she knew that this was their only hope at a lasting happiness. Dr. Wills was also sad to see them go. He had come to love John as the son he never had.

He was so proud of John's abilities as a doctor. John soaked up knowledge like a sponge, but he was also a good teacher. John had brought Mr. Wong Lee's knowledge of herbs to him and he was very grateful for that knowledge. John's departure would leave a big hole in his heart and in the community as a whole, but he also recognized the continued risk to the young couple if they stayed.

The small caravan grew considerably when Sergeant O'Malley showed up with six loaded-down mules in tow. Then every ones eyes bugged when the store keeper arrived with six more heavily loaded mules. This made quite a spectacle. There were four mounts, and when John added his own mule that was loaded with medicines, camping gear, personal items, and food, the caravan now included 13 mules, 4 horses, four laying hens, a Road Island red rooster, and the Sergeant's seven sled dogs.

Once they were ready to depart, Thunder Heart, Mari, and Billy were met with handshakes and hugs. Saying goodbye was hard for everyone. Billy smiled and thanked Nelly for being very decent to him and his mother.

Nelly tearfully gave Billy some extra money and some extra sweet cakes to take with, but Billy refused the money saying, "Thanks Ms. Nelly, but I won't be needin' money where we is goin'. I would ask a favor of ya, though."

"Yes, Billy, anythin'," said Nelly. "What be it child?"

"Would ya put some flowers on me ma's grave once a year fer me?"

Nelly smiled and hugged him tight, and as tears streamed down her face she replied, "Oh my good Lord, yes, child. Ya have me word."

"Thanks, Ms. Nelly. I'll miss ya and the mister."

"Well, we'll be missin' ya too, Billy." With one last hug and a quick well-placed kiss to his forehead, she bid him farewell and he mounted his horse.

As Mari sat atop her horse observing Nelly and Billy, she began to wonder.

Billy's mother had been a good woman and had been used badly by men all her life. This started Mari thinking hard about how her life would turn out. She knew she loved Thunder Heart with all her heart, but would she end up like Billy's mom if he died? Seeing her deep in thought, Thunder laid his hand on her shoulder and smiled. "Don't worry, *mitawin*. You will never be alone. My family is quite large. You will never be alone as Bella was."

She smiled back at him sweetly, always amazed at his perceptiveness. Billy eager to get under way said, "Let's get a move on, folks. We're burning daylight." Then he kicked Star into motion.

And as he rode out ahead of them, smiling broadly, they all laughed and kicked their mounts into a trot. Their new life awaited them. They followed Billy through town but soon Thunder took the lead to set the pace, and Will brought up the rear with the chickens swaying and clucking atop a mule and the dogs barking, all leashed together and trailing along behind him. They made quite a parade as they rode through town, but even though there were still jeers and taunts, there were also waves and fond farewells too.

They rode on until dusk before making camp in a sunny meadow by a small stream. John and the sergeant, worrying that bandits may have followed them from town, decided that they shouldn't make a fire that first night. They ate a cold meal of sandwiches and Nelly's cookies, and Billy bedded down beside Mari under the sheltering arms of an old oak. Thunder felt the hairs prickling the back of his neck, as if he were being watched by many pairs of eyes. Speaking in whispers with Will, they decided that perhaps a small fire was needed after all to ward off wolves from the live stock as long as they traded on and off watch. Will bundled himself in a red and black trade blanket and took the first watch while Thunder Heart built a small fire and bedded down next to Mari.

Mari and Billy were asleep as soon as their heads hit the covers and didn't see Thunder making a false bed for Will who walked off to sit guard and watch over them from the bushes. It was around one am when Will woke Thunder to take his turn at watch, but before he lay down, he told his lead dog to guard. Will O'Malley felt safer knowing that there were two good guards on duty.

Thunder Heart had heard wolves singing in the night. He knew wolves did not usually attack people, but he would remain on his guard just in case. However, relying on the sled dogs to alert him of dangers, he drifted on and off, waking quickly at the slightest sound.

Thunder woke the others at dawn to break camp and head out. However, he couldn't shake the feeling that they were in danger when so close to the white man's world. He covered their trail while Will loaded several rifles, even giving one to Billy and Mari. The others he divided between Thunder and himself. When they departed camp, they took a rarely-traveled and steeper trail toward the mountain pass.

They hadn't ridden very far when a shot rang out, and Thunder felt a bullet whiz past his head. He ducked down and yelled for everyone to dismount and run for cover behind some large boulders nearby. Thunder, quickly making sure Mari and Billy were unhurt and well-covered, tossed them their rifles and told them to remain hidden while he circled around to try and get behind the shooters. Mari was terrified and her hand shook so badly she could hardly hold the heavy gun, but she pulled herself together knowing Thunder needed her help to protect Billy and the horses. Will fired a few shots in the direction the shots had been fired from in order to draw the focus away from Thunder as he moved, and to also show him just where the shooter or shooters were.

On silent feet, Thunder picked his way through the terrain, ducking behind boulders and trees as he went. Finally when he was close enough to see their attackers, he was filled with rage. It was no other than the hate-filled Radner. Thunder had heard that the man had escaped from the constables while being transferred to prison to await hanging. He had hoped however, that the man had been caught or shot by now, but here he was again attempting to harm his family.

When he saw Radner fire a shot in Mari's direction, he yelled out, "Hold it right there, you filthy bastard!"

Radner, hearing the command, swung around and stood up to fire, but Will, seeing a good target, fired first and the outlaw died instantly from a bullet through the heart. Radner dropped like a sack of potatoes tumbling down the hillside to the rocks below. Thunder nodded his thanks to Will before he faded into the trees to see if there were any other bandits with Radner.

Finding no one else, he took Radner's horse from where it was tied and walked back to where the others remained hidden. Mari, upon seeing him safe and unharmed, rushed into his arms. He held her tenderly for a long while, whispering softly to her in Cheyenne. When she finally stopped shaking they remounted and continued on their way, leaving Radner's body to return to the earth where he fell.

They rode steadily onwards after that, stopping briefly a few times to rest and water the horses, answer nature's call, and snack on honey cakes and jerky, which they washed down with cool, fresh water. That evening, they made camp beside a blazing fire, and having feasted on a meal of roasted rabbit and bathed in a nearby stream, they fell asleep early underneath a myriad of sparkling stars.

The next day the weather turned cold and rainy. They had been steadily ascending in elevation and by evening they were soaked through, cold, and hungry. With well-learned skill and a lot of luck, Thunder Heart found them a small cave where he left William, Billy and Mari to set up camp and build a fire while he hunted for their supper. That evening they feasted on a stew of rabbit and wild greens that he had dug up along his way. John worried about Mari, as she was unaccustomed to long hours in the saddle, and though she did not complain, he brewed a healing tea for her and held her close as they sat by the fire.

His blood burned for her. He could smell the lilac perfume she used, and with each breath he took, it filled his soul with desire. He wanted to taste her sweetness and yearned to burying himself in her depth. He imagined her response to him as he kissed her and he sighed deeply. He could not get her to his home quickly enough for his peace of mind. He hugged her close and placed a soft kiss on the top of her head as she dozed off in his arms. Once asleep, he laid her down on the firs and covered her with his buffalo robe.

Billy sat by the fire, braiding a length of leather. He wanted to make it into a new bridle for his horse, one that didn't use a bit. The old nag had bad teeth and was not worth much, but to Billy, she was the greatest thing ever. He had spent hours brushing and combing her until her coat was soft and shiny. He fed her sweet grass he had cut himself just for her and the horse loved the boy.

Thunder Heart, taking in the sight of his new family, found his heart swelling with love and pride. He felt in the depths of his being that he was the richest of men. After tossing another log on the fire, he started telling Billy the history of the Cheyenne people and how his tribe had come to live in the mountain valley that they now called home. William was already asleep when Billy noticed Thunder Heart's fatigue and piped up.

"Sir, I know ya and the Sergeant didn't sleep so good last night sittin' guard an' all. So if in ya don't mind, I'll sit here and keep watch fir awhile. You can sleep next to Mari and keep her warm. If I sees or hears anythin' outta place, I'll gets ya up, okay?"

"Okay, Billy," replied Thunder. "Wake me when the moon gets

high, and thanks."

Billy smiled to himself as Thunder Heart slid under the robe and pulled Mari close. He fell asleep almost instantly.

By the middle of the night, he woke up with a jerk, all too aware of the softness he cradled in his arms. He shook the sleep from his head, ran his fingers through his tangled hair, and laid another log on the fire before relieving a very tired Billy.

Thunder, upon rising, realized that the rain had stopped, even though he still heard the steady drip, drip, drip of moisture running off the rocks. Feeling a chill, he wrapped himself in a trade blanket, poured a cup of coffee, and took his position at the mouth of the cave for what would be the remainder of the night.

As he sat in the cave's mossy entrance, staring up at the vast expanse of stars, he thought that they looked like they had been cast across the heavens like sparkling jewels on a blanket of black velvet. He had always found comfort in the knowledge that *Ma'heo'o* was indeed mighty and full of wisdom. He remembered how in the beginning of all things, *Ma'heo'o* had asked mother spider to spin an unseen web in the heavens upon which he hung the camp fires of the ancestors. Then he constructed the awesome Sky Road that lead the departed souls to their eternal happiness. As he gazed at the beauty of *Hanhepi-wi* (Moon Woman) he began softly chanting his prayers, asking *Ma'heo'o* for the strength needed to preserve his honor and keep them all safe.

The next morning, the sun broke over the mountains in a blaze of golden glory. Thunder Heart raised his eyes skyward as he heard the cry of a red-tailed hawk. Suddenly fearing the bird was his father's, he was filled with dread and whistled a call to the bird, but the bird did not return it. It just flew away. He smiled then as he became aware of the sense of peace that again filled his heart.

More relaxed and rested now, they all set out again, anticipating a more enjoyable journey. But by evening, Mari had developed a slight cough, and Thunder was becoming worried with each passing mile that an infection was settling into her chest. When they made camp, he brewed her some tea made from stinging nettle and willow bark, and they all got a good laugh at the faces and complaints she gave as she drank it down. The next morning, Mari awakened refreshed and her cough was gone.

Days and nights past, and they fell into a relaxed routine with each day ending with the telling of stories: stories from the Bible and stories about *Ma'heo'o*; stories about the mighty hero twins and how they battled and killed the giant monsters that once lived on the earth, enabling people to live in safety. He also told the story of his uncle, Little Beaver, of how as a small boy, he had followed a mighty warrior into the land of the grandmother, and how he survived with his friends until they were found by Quiet Hawk, Thunder Heart's father, and how as a small boy, Beaver helped save the horses and the people from the great fire that destroyed Dream Valley, their western valley home.

Each night, Thunder Heart's heart swelled with joy as he beheld the rapped faces of Mari, Billy, and Will. He liked telling stories and often used sign language to embellish them.

Often William would tell his own tales of life as a Mountie. Catching bad guys and living in the wilderness. Thunder Heart knew that Will would be a great asset to their tribal community with his knowledge of engineering and farming and hoped that he might even find a woman to take as a wife. Every man deserved a family, even a son of his own to teach.

The closer to home they got, the more Thunder missed his family— Winter Blue in particular— and the words of the White Buffalo, about fighting a battle with a sickness that had already begun, haunted him.

On the evening before they reached Dream Valley, Thunder Heart heard the cry of a mountain lion, and it sounded close. He knew that Billy was off taking care of the stock so he alerted Will, and they grabbed their weapons. The next thing they heard was Billy screaming and they took off running. When they got to the boy, the big cat was poised over Billy with its teeth bared, ready to rip out the boy's throat.

Billy was fighting well, though. He had already plunged the knife Thunder Heart had given him deep into the cat's side and was successfully holding the big cat away from his throat, but his strength was waning. William raised his rifle and shot true, dropping the animal instantly. Thunder Heart dragged the big male cat off of Billy and looked him over for injuries. Billy was visibly shaken and sported several deep scratches on his chest. Thunder Heart would clean them well and apply a poultice, allowing the wounds to heal from the inside-out. Cats held lots of foul things in their claws, and the wounds they left tended to become infected easily.

It took both men to drag the cat carcass far away from their camp. The meat would feed the dogs and the predators of the forest, but Thunder decided to keep the hide because it clearly showed that Billy had bravely stabbed the animal and fought well.

The next day, Thunder set a grueling pace in hopes of making the valley by nightfall and rode far in the lead of the others.

Billy didn't let his injuries slow him down any, and he didn't complain even once. He was trying so hard to show his new father and Will that he was a man, that no one knew he was really sick, until the boy fell off his horse.

"John, Will, it's Billy!" cried Mari.

They all dismounted and rushed to the child. He was burning up with fever. Mari retrieved her canteen and started washing Billy's face while the men made camp. It had been looking like rain all day so they set up two big lean-tos.

Once Billy was settled in one, and his clothes were removed, John could see that the cause of the trouble was due to the closing of one of the deeper scratches. It was a good thing Billy was unconscious because he would have to reopen the wound to drain out the poison. Will gritted his teeth while Thunder, using a hot knife, slit the boy's skin and was sickened by the awful that drained out. Then he used hot salt water to clean the wound and he even cut away some of the infected tissue before applying a poultice of comfrey and marigold.

Thunder Heart left camp to hunt up some supper while William tended the stock and gathered up more fire wood. William had found a stream close by and brought Mari a large kettle of fresh, cool water to use to bathe Billy with in hopes of decreasing his fever. Billy awakened after an hour or two, and Mari was able to get some willow bark tea down him before he drifted back off to sleep.

The weather did indeed turn cool and rainy that night. Will shooed Mari out of Billy's lean-to and settled in with the boy for the night.

Mari and John snuggled in their own lean-to, caressing each other under their warm buffalo robe. They rested on their sides like spoons, and he interred her from behind while his long fingers caressed her folds. She wanted to cry out her release, but as John felt her muscles tighten around him, he turned her head and captured her cries with a deep, passionate kiss. Mari wanted to turn and hold him, but he continued to possess her, and she fell asleep safe within his loving embrace.

The next morning, the warm sunlight burst through the trees in golden streamers that transformed the forest into a beautiful fairyland. Mari prepared a breakfast of fry bread, bacon and coffee, and Billy woke up hungry.

They stayed there for two more days before starting out again.

Thunder Heart had worried about Mari not being able to endure the wilderness life, but she literally blossomed before his eyes, and on the morning she had awakened, nauseated and unable to eat her breakfast, he finally understood why.

Thunder followed her into the bushes and held her hair for her while she emptied the contents of her stomach. When she finished, she blushed her embarrassment as he wiped her face with a cool rag he had brought from camp.

"I'm so sorry, John, that I'm such a bother," she apologized. "I can't figure out why I'm so sick. I've been a little nauseated of late, but I thought it would pass."

Thunder looked into her beautiful, yet sad eyes, and enfolded her within the warmth of his strong arms. He kissed the top of her head and rested a hand on her belly. "*Mitawin*, you are not sick, you're pregnant."

Mari gasped, "P-pregnant, but how… OH..? My monthly, oh my. It's been one, maybe two months since my last monthly." She suddenly beamed and threw her arms around Thunder's neck and kissed him wildly before she squealed, "We're going to have a baby!" Thunder, so affected by her joy, picked her up and swung her around as they both broke out into joyous laughter. When they returned back to camp, they were greeted with heart-filled congratulations from William and Billy.

Will searched through his pack and brought her some soda bread to eat on while Thunder brewed her some ginger tea.

Later that day, Mari requested them to stop so she could pick some blackberries she'd seen, telling the men she would make them some fried pies to eat with their supper. Not wanting to delay their journey much more, they all picked berries and when she felt they had enough, they continued on. Thunder chuckled to himself at her purple lips and wondered if her kisses would taste like berries.

CHAPTER 31: COMING HOME

To Thunder Heart, it seemed it was taking an extra long time to get home, but in reality, not counting the incident with Billy and the lion, and not wanting to overtax Mari, they had made good time.

Mari had gained strength and stamina over the journey, and even though she had developed a slight cough in the beginning from sleeping on the ground, it was no longer a problem. Billy healed rapidly and even helped now with the hunting. It made Thunder very proud to know that this child would do well in his family.

The day that they reached Dream Valley, Thunder spotted a hawk riding the wind high above them. He raised his hand and let out with a shrill whistle. The great red-tailed hawk gave a shrill cry and dove downward to land on Thunder Heart's outstretched arm. The others, sitting atop their mounts, watched wide-eyed, awed by the wonder of what they saw. Thunder petted the bird a while before taking a small, blue string from his medicine bag. He tied the string to the bird's foot and then tossed it skyward. They watched as the mighty bird rose higher and higher into the sky, but it didn't continue to fly as if hunting. Instead, it circled above them once and then headed due east.

Billy was so excited he could barely sit still. "W-was that your father's hawk?" he asked.

"Yes Billy, but the bird doesn't belong to my father," Thunder Heart stated. "They are brothers. Two halves of the same spirit. Cha'ta will go and tell my father that we are coming so the tribe will be ready when we ride in."

"But how did he know we were here, and how did he even know where to look for us?" asked Mari.

William chuckled and said, "That bird hunts this area all the time."

"Not to make light of what you have said, Will, but there is more to it than that," stated Thunder. "My Great Uncle probably saw our coming in a dream days ago and sent the bird to find us."

"Really?" Billy asked.

"Yes, Billy," Thunder Heart stated, "My Great Uncle Quiet Waters is the best vision dreamer of our tribe and his dreams have always been true. You will all understand when we finally get there."

Before long, they reached the ridgeline above the most beautiful valley Mari had ever seen.

"Is this where you live, John?" asked Mari.

"No," said Thunder. "Do you remember me telling you the story of my grandfather's dream and the valley he and my people found?" The others nodded in unison. "Well, this is Dream Valley, and from what I see, the water in the river is down."

"Why is that important Thunder?" Will asked. "Aren't we a goin' up and over the pass, me boy?"

"You have been gone many years, Uncle. The people got together and constructed a road along the river to connect both valleys. Now only a day of pleasant riding separates both places. Our population is growing and this valley is perfect for farming while Mist Valley is better for raising livestock."

As they descended to the valley floor, William's brain set itself to racing.

"Thunder, me boy, I can see this place becomin' a sweet little farmin' town in no time at all, with a store, a grist mill by the river, a smithy and livery over there, and even a doctor's office among the trees there. We can be a buildin' a saw mill right over yonder." He pointed at a spot farther down river. "That way we could be havein' it all built in no time."

"Yes," Mari piped in. "We can build a school and even a hospital."

"Hey, don't be forgittin' the newspaper and the telegraph office, sir," Billy said.

Thunder chuckled. "Alright, all of you. You seem to be forgetting the stories I told you. This Valley doesn't fully belong to us any longer."

"No, it doesn't," Will stated firmly, but the broad smile on his face betrayed his rough reply. "I own it!!" He said before bursting out laughing. "I've been a bustin' to be tellin' ye, me boy, this whole blessed trip. I sold all of me property in Vancouver and purchased the whole wide valley, and since I have no other kin I put the deed in me own and yer family's name. Now yer people own it free and clear, and as fer me, me boy, I can't wait ta get ta buildin'."

Thunder was overcome with gratitude. His eyes misted over and he stated with a lump in his throat, "Uncle William, my heart has no words to express my joy and gratitude to you. I can not wait to tell my grandfather that Dream Valley is ours once again. Let's ride."

They rode excitedly along the new river road, until Thunder turned off onto a path that gradually ascended the mountain through a thick old growth forest that consisted of a mixture of conifers and broad leaf trees.

Thunder took a deep breath, savoring the woodsy smell. "Ahhh," he sighed. "It smells like home."

William too took a deep breath. "Aye, me boy, that it does, that it does."

"Home always has a smell that is sacred to a person's soul, one that when smelled, automatically gives a person a sense of peace," Thunder explained as they rode.

Mari sighed also before commenting, "Home to me smells like lavender and honeysuckle and roses with just a hint of pigs."

"Pigs?" replied Billy.

"Yes, pigs. My mother had a beautiful flower garden next to the house by our bedrooms, and the smell of the flowers would come through the open windows and fill the whole house, and I had a pet sow named Bess who lived by our barn out back. And even though we kept her pin as clean as we could, there was always just a hint of pig on the breeze. My grandfather would laugh at me when I complained about the smell and say that it just smelled like money to him. He would breed her and sell the piglets for a tidy profit."

Billy just got a sad look on his face and grew quieter as they rode on. He thought of what home smelled like to him, and sadly realized that it smelled like his mom.

They rode steadily upward until nightfall, and finally made camp in a beautiful misty glade.

Thunder Heart held Mari tenderly in his arms as they lay by the fire. They watched the flames lap hungrily at the dead fall, and Mari snuggled closer as she watched the sparks lift skyward in the wind. She had the feeling they were carrying her prayers and dreams to the Cheyenne campfires above.

Thunder Heart, however, was not so calmly contented. The feelings that Mari stirred in him made his heart beat like a thunder drum. And though he was filled with need and want, he could not bring himself to make love to her tonight. They had set a very fast pace today, riding many hard miles, and he didn't want to irritate her body further and risk the life she carried within her womb. So he just lay there holding his greatest treasure while the others slept on. When Mari sighed, turned over, and wrapped her arms and legs about him, he had to grit his teeth to control his rising discomfort. He wanted to move, readjusting to a more comfortable position, but instead he took a long deep breath, sighed, and continued to hold her. After a while when he heard her slow, rhythmic breathing, and knew she was deeply asleep, he moved slightly.

When he had freed an arm, he reached up and brushed the hair from her face and whispered softly, "Tomorrow my love. Tomorrow." Then he kissed her cheek before pulling the blankets over her small shoulders. He loved her with all of his being, and while she slept, with her head on his chest, he placed his hand gently upon her abdomen. He was so very tired but it was only when he heard the howl of a lone wolf that he finally felt safe enough to relax. He was home, and he fell asleep praying for good health and safety for his beloved and their child.

CHAPTER 32: JOYFUL ACCEPTANCE

The next day, when they rode into the small village town of Mist Valley, they were greeted by a throng of friends and relatives, headed up by his parents. Mari could understand now why John had insisted they put on their best clothes prior to arrival, but Thunder just wore his buckskins, looking fully Indian once more. John Thunder Heart was a handsome man in whatever he wore, but Mari thought she liked his Indian attire best of all. He looked so regal, she thought with his eagle feather dancing proudly in the wind as it hung tied into a single long braid that hung behind his right ear.

His parents were an impressive couple also, and there seemed to be strength of character about them that Mari couldn't quite fathom. Thunder reached up and helped her from her mount and walked her over to them.

She smiled sweetly as he introduced her as his wife, and she was surprised by the warm hugs that she received from them.

Quiet Hawk, still holding her hand, turned to his son and said, "She is a fine woman, my son. We will ready the sweat lodge for the purification and dreaming ceremony so you can be wed at the full moon that comes in two days."

"Father, she can not go through the sweat lodge ceremony," he said before glancing down into her questioning eyes, then back up to his father's. "She is already with child." Seeing the worried look on his beloved father's face, he continued saying, "Do not worry A'te. I followed all the proper rituals, and while we were wed in the white man's way, we mated under the light of *Epanewi's* (the moon's) new light. I do not know why *Ma'heo'o* chose her for me, but she completes my spirit."

Before Helee could engulf her new daughter-in-law in a motherly hug, a booming voice came from the crowd.

"I know why the Great Spirit chose her, my Grand nephew," replied an elderly man that headed toward them. Mari watched as a hunched, frail-looking man with white hair streaming past his shoulders walked slowly toward them. Using a tall walking stick— from which hung many feathers— to lean upon, the Elder came to stand before them. Quiet Waters, smiling knowingly, reached out and took one of Mari's trembling hands before looking directly into her eyes. Mari was overcome with the feeling that the elder Shaman could see right into her very soul. When she blushed and dropped her eyes, he patted her hand softly. He smiled at Thunder before stating, "She is the daughter of a Suquamish princess. I saw her parents in a dream."

Mari looked inquisitively at Quiet Waters before stating, "You must be Quiet Waters. I am so pleased to meet you. John, I mean, Thunder Heart, has told me so much about you. I always knew my mother was different from the other women in town, but I knew nothing of her heritage. All I ever knew about her life was that she loved my father very much. She never talked about her past. Thank you Grandfather, for telling me."

Quiet Waters was very pleased that Mari had used the respectful term of Grandfather when speaking to him, and with eyes sparkling with mirth, he stated, "You are most welcome my granddaughter."

With this knowledge from Quiet Waters, the pieces of Mari's life fell into place, helping her to finally relax within the arms of her husband's people. She was Indian too, and she felt a peaceful sense of belonging spread throughout her heart.

"Now, where is this Blue Hawk I have been seeing?" asked Quiet Waters.

Billy came forward now along with retired Sergeant O'Malley.

"I am Blue Hawk, sir," he said as he took the elder's leathery, thin hand.

Quiet Waters held Billy's hand firmly, and stated loudly so everyone could hear, "Everyone this is Mahomet's Blue Hawk and he will grow to do great things for our people."

Billy blushed as he was engulfed in warm hugs and pats of welcome. When the people finally stopped greeting him, he noticed a boy about his age walking up to them. Mari saw him too, and touched Thunder's arm to get his attention. Following her gaze, Thunder Heart saw his son and motioned him over. The boy walked over to him quickly and embraced his father warmly.

"I have missed you, A'te. You were gone a very long time. Uncle Beaver took me hunting and I killed my first deer seven days ago."

"Congratulations, my son," Thunder beamed. "Has my son become a man while I was gone?"

"No, A'te, not yet. I have not yet sought my vision. I waited for you."

Thunder Heart's eyes misted and again hugged his son.

"I am home now, and here I will remain. When you are ready to seek your vision, we will go together." Winter Blue's smile spread like sunshine across his face. Then Thunder Heart introduced him to Mari and William before he introduced him to Billy.

"Winter Blue, this is Billy Blue Hawk. I have taken him into our family. I hope you will help me teach him our ways. He has no other family and I have come to look upon him also as a son."

Winter looked at his father, then at Billy, and back to his father again, before saying, "That's great, A'te, I always wanted a brother. I'll show him where we put the horses and introduce him to the other boys." The boys departed then at a run, the mounts in tow.

Next to come forward was a tall Indian in priestly robes who hugged John warmly. Mari could not contain herself and blurted out, "You're Father Black Crow?"

"Yes daughter, I am. Quiet Hawk, Quiet Waters and I keep and protect the hearts and spirits of our people here."

Smiling sweetly as her embarrassment spread over her entire body, she said "John... I mean... Thunder Heart has told me so much about all of you that I feel that I know you all already."

Helee and Quiet Hawk frowned and said, "John? Why does she call you John, Thunder Heart?"

"Forgive me, my parents," Thunder Heart replied. "I found it necessary to take a white name while I was living among the whites, but enough of this talk for now. We will tell you all everything you wish to know around the fire later tonight."

Quiet Hawk, seeing the boys returning, signaled for Billy to come forward. Billy shyly walked up to stand before Quiet Hawk, but he didn't speak. Quiet Hawk smiled gently at the boy and patted him on the shoulder and said, "I am Thunder Heart's father, and I wanted to welcome you among us my grandson."

Billy's eyes filled with tears and he whispered softly, "I've never had a grandfather, sir, and I have never lived with Indians before. The other boys know so much more than I do. It makes me feel stupid."

Quiet Hawk took the boy gently in his arms and whispered softly into the boy's ear, "Don't worry, Billy. We will all teach you everything you need to know to live a long and happy life among us."

Billy was so overcome by the gentleness of this man that he hugged Quiet Hawk fiercely. Then he suddenly let go and ran back to his horse. Hugging its neck, he whispered into the horse's ear, "I have a grandfather. Isn't it wonderful?"

The horse nodded her head as if it understood every word. Everyone smiled and Thunder Heart couldn't suppress the chuckle that rose up within him, at seeing his small friend's happiness.

Sergeant O'Malley held back from the welcoming family, but Lean Elk, Thunder Heart's step grandfather and elder tribal Chief, greeted him warmly.

"I am so glad to see you again my brother," he stated. "But why do you not wear the clothes of the Mounties?"

"I have resigned my post, and I wish to ask the council if I can settle in Dream Valley. I have brought many things with me and I wish to help your people to resettle the valley and build a small farming town. Will you help me bring my ideas to the council?"

"I will be honored to do so. Many of our people have expressed a desire to return now that the road along the river has been completed."

The men walked to the council house in the center of the village while the boys took all the animals and their cargo to the community livery where the supplies would be stored and the live stock could be cared for.

Mari was so warmly welcomed by Thunder Heart's family and tribe that she could hardly believe it. Helee, Thunder's mother, and John's sisters took her to the Hot Springs as soon as they had gotten their things settled. She soaked and savored in the wonderful warm water while Helee asked her lots of questions of a personal nature.

Mari blushed deeply, but answered every question without hesitation.

"There was a great storm at sea," she told them. "And I was swept from the ship by a giant wave. I couldn't fight the waves and the cold, and then blackness took me. John's face was the first I saw when I awoke. I vaguely remember his strong arms holding me close and warming me. I was so cold and my worry for my brother was all-consuming. John's gentle hands, as well as his nasty-tasting teas, saved my life, but my beloved brother perished."

"I am so sorry, Mari, about your brother," Helee said. "But I am glad my son was there to save you. Do you truly love him?"

"Yes, I love him with all my heart. I think I fell in love with him the moment my eyes locked with his. I felt like he looked directly into my soul. And when he touches me, my heart beats so fast that I lose my breath and I feel warm and tingly deep inside."

Heat flooded Mari's cheeks as she blushed a deep scarlet when John's sister asked if she had been a maiden.

"Yes. I was until our wedding night," Mari replied her head held high. "John was very honorable and took such good care of me. We have been together day and night since he found me on the beach. He protected my honor and I wore white at our wedding."

Helee looked at Mari approvingly and said, "It is good that you decided to wed my son. You see, according to the old traditions of our people, if a man and woman slept within the same dwelling or even shared a blanket they were considered married."

"OH!" Mari gasped, raising her hand to her cheek. "I do love him, but was he just marrying me to save my honor? I really thought he loved me." She hung her head sadly, and Helee took her into her arms.

"Child, he loves you. I saw this in his eyes when he looked at you."

Mari brightened and sunk lower in the water, sighing with relief. Hoping to change the subject, she stated, "This water feels so wonderful."

"Yes, and it will purify you." Helee washed Mari's hair and John's sister rubbed sage and herbs into it and over her whole body. Helee told her that this was to prepare her for their wedding ceremony that would take place tonight after the welcoming feast. Mari's eyes widened.

Helee smiled with a knowing smile, and stated. "It is our custom to wed under the first full moon of the month. If it is not tonight, you will have to wait until the next moon before you can share a bed together. And I do not think my son wants to wait. In fact, I think he planned to arrive here on this day because even now he is in the sweat lodge with his father, grandfather, Black Crow, and Quiet Waters preparing himself both physically and spiritually for what is to come. There will be a feast and dance, and my son will tell our people why he has chosen you. Then he will call you to him and you will say your vows to each other as you stand before the faces of *Ma'heo'o* and *Hanhepi'wi*."

Mari felt the butterflies growing within her stomach and looked a little downcast again. "I wish I had thought to make a special dress for the service. I do have the nice one I wore for our first service. Will that do?"

"No, my daughter. You will wear the one that we have made for you." Mari looked at Helee with a puzzled expression. Helee dipped back down into the warm waters and said, "Let's soak some more."

"Mari," Helee started. "I knew that someday Thunder Heart would marry, and so I made a dress for his bride. But it was not used at his first wedding. It has been waiting for you and only you since he described you to me. You see, he saw you in a dream during his first vision quest and test of manhood. He did not know the meaning of the vision then, but I knew that the spirits and *Ma'heo'o* would lead you to him when the time was right, as they led his father to me many years ago."

After about an hour of soaking, a small girl ran to them, full of excitement. "Grandmother, Grandfather says you must come now and prepare."

"Thank you, Early Dawn, we will come right away," Helee replied.

The women got out of the spring and wrapped themselves in blankets before quickly following the child back to Helee's cabin. The cabin was warm, and as they dried by the fire, Helee brushed Mari's long hair until it was silky and tangle-free. After a short time, Quiet Waters entered the cabin after announcing himself and sprinkled sage and sweet grass into the fire. He handed a smoking wooden bowl of the herbs to Helee and after the old shaman left, she passed the bowl over and around to Mari. Then she had her stand with her legs spread, and Helee passed the smoking bowl between her legs, six times.

"Now, my daughter," she said. "You are pure and blessed by the spirits. *Ma'heo'o* will bless you and my son with many children."

Mari, blushing, laid her hand over the slight swell of her stomach. Thunder heart's sister brought forth a bundle and handed it to Helee, and Mari's mouth hung open when the package was unfolded. It was a white doeskin dress with long fringes at the hem, sides, arms, and bodice. It was decorated with elk teeth and elaborate beading and dried porcupine quills. The design on the back was one of a buffalo standing under a lightning-streaked sky. Also, repeated across the entire front of the bodice was the Cheyenne star pattern, colored in the sacred colors of the six sacred directions; red, blue, green, yellow, white, and black. There were also knee-high white moccasins beaded in the same star pattern and lightning bolt design. After Mari was dressed, and a medallion in the form of the star was placed in her hair along with fluffy white feathers, she was ushered out to the main campfire where Quiet Hawk was singing and beating his hand drum. As the women stopped before the huge crackling bonfire, Mari beheld Thunder Heart in all of his finest.

He was magnificent— dressed in a long, white, beaded breech clout. His upper arms were adorned with golden bands and his raven black hair was adorned with a beaded clasp and a single eagle feather. Upon his shoulders, he wore the sacred White Buffalo robe that had been decorated with a large Cheyenne star made from dried porcupine quills. Black Crow, standing next to him, reached up with his hand to quiet the people who had been trilling loudly.

When Thunder Heart beheld Mari, he gasped and his knees nearly buckled. Tears glistened in his eyes and his mouth suddenly went dry. He could hardly believe that this vision he beheld was his Mari. This was the woman he had seen on his first vision quest. It was an overwhelming feeling for him to know that the spirits were right and true, and also a relief to know that the spirits had given their blessing and direction to his life so long ago. He silently thanked them for his Mari, and then as she approached, he sang the song of his heart. Mari stood spellbound. She did not understand his words, but Helee repeated them to her as they walked together to stand beside him.

"Behold, oh Ma'heo'o," he sang. "Spirits of the Buffalo and the four winds, Mother Earth and Father Sky behold the woman you have given to me. She is a vision most fair, and has a heart that is pure and good and true. Behold, all my people, she is my Heart Song.

She holds the light of my love in her eyes and my heart is in her hands. I am made strong with her at my side, and this I swear will be so forever."

Sweet, silent tears of joy slid down Mari's cheeks as Helee whispered the words to her. Mari loved Thunder, with all her heart. Before anyone could stop her, she turned and faced his people and stated, "Behold this great man who is strong in body and gentle in spirit, a mighty man of honor and healing who is kind to all living things. I, Mari, who was orphaned by the great sea, am unworthy of him."

She heard him gasp, then turning, she gazed up at him and took hold of his hands. She looked deeply into his eyes and smiled softly, before continuing.

"But Thunder Heart of the Cheyenne, I love you with all of my heart and soul. I will stand at your side and give you many children. You are all the family I need. You are my life now and forever."

Silent tears filled the eyes of all the people. Many had not liked the fact that their healer had taken a woman who had white blood as his wife, but now they saw and heard the rightness of it.

Black Crow spoke now: "In the name of the great spirit, his son Jesus, and their Holy Spirit that fills all living things. I ask blessing upon these two whom the Spirits have brought together and caused their hearts to be with love. Amen."

He made the sign of the cross above their heads, and took their joined hands and wrapped a soft cord around them.

Then Quiet Hawk spoke as he smudged them with sacred smoke. "You are now no longer two, but one. You will never know cold, because one will be warmth for the other. You will share the same joys and sadness and be strength for each other. You will be forever bound as lovers in this world and the next. This is the will of *Ma'heo'o* and the White Buffalo spirit."

Quiet Hawk, directing his gaze and speech now to all the people stated, "I can say this because just this morning before they arrived, Beaver told me he saw the White Buffalo again among the herd."

The people began shouting and trilling, hugging each other because the prophecy given to Thunder Heart so long ago had come true and their people had been truly blessed by *Ma'heo'o*, the Creator.

CHAPTER 33: A PROPHECY COMPLETED

Thunder's heart soared with so much joy that he grabbed Mari around the thighs, lifted her high, hugged her close, and declared loudly, "You are mine for always, Mari. Always!"

He then placed a kiss on her abdomen and slid her down the hard length of his body to claim her lips in a kiss so deep with passion that it almost made her swoon. Her heart was beating so hard and fast that she just knew he must be feeling it because he was holding her so close.

The feast was wonderful, and Mari was so overwhelmed by everyone. The women bustled around serving food as the children danced around the central fire and Mari was spellbound as the men beat the thunder drum and danced with all their hearts. Even Thunder joined in and she felt her heart flutter with desire at the graceful power of his steps and leaps.

When the party was over, John and Mari barely heard the shouts of congratulations and shrill trilling as they walked hand-in-hand to the large cabin that would be their new home. Mari hardly noticed the warm fire or the flowers, or even the soft firs. So consumed was she by the fires of passion as he claimed her lips with his, that moisture pooled between her legs. John tenderly and slowly placed kisses on her face, and trailed them down her neck, before burying his face in her silken hair. She smelled of flowers, sage and woman, and his body responded with overwhelming need and desire. As she rested her arms around his neck, he reached up and pulled the ties at the shoulders of her dress, letting it fall to the floor. Then he ran his trembling hands over her skin, finally settling one hand on a firm breast, caressing and teasing her nipple with his thumb. Once it hardened to a taught peak, he bent and claimed it with his lips, sending such a hot tingling sensation spreading through her, that she shivered with delight.

He stooped down on one knee before her, and trailed hot licks and kisses across her stomach, to her mound. And after stopping to savor her womanhood, he continued down her legs until he reached her ankles where he stopped to remove her moccasins. She placed her hands on his shoulders to keep her balance as he reached up to grasp her bottom, pulling her womanhood again to his awaiting lips. She mewed and moaned as he kissed her there, parting her soft folds with his tongue and suckling on her distended nub. She threw her head back and thought she would fly apart as he made love to her with his mouth.

He held her to him with one arm and reached up with his other to fondle her breast, and as he lightly pinched her nipple, he felt her tremble. Then as he flicked his tongue rhythmically over her nub, he heard her cry out her orgasm. Pulling her down to him after that, he laid her back onto the firs and rose above her. Smiling roguishly, he licked his lips, savoring the taste of her. She was so sweet, so right, and she was all his. While Mari lay there catching her breath, he reached over to a bag of sage that sat by the hearth and sprinkled it into the fire. As the dwelling again filled with the sacred fragrance, Mari's mind was being clouded with passion as she languidly beheld her husband's naked, fully-aroused body. Her heart pounded within her, and she felt the heat and tingling of desire begin again between her thighs.

Her husband, she thought as she looked at him, was magnificent, with his broad shoulders and well-muscled lean body. Her eyes traveled the length of him before settling on his manhood. It stood out proudly before him, long and thick, and she wanted him fully. As the passion built within her, she was overwhelmed with the need to feel him inside her. She wanted him to be a part of her now and always.

Thunder heart descended upon her, pulling her close to the hard length of him. As he drew her into his arms, he could feel her rapid heartbeat under his lips as he kissed her neck. Wrapping his fingers in her long tresses, he brushed his lips over hers. She opened her lips and reached up, putting her arms around his neck and deepened their kiss. As Thunder Heart plundered her sweetness, he had to remind himself to go slow, but he didn't know if he could hold off long enough. It would take all of his control to make this joining as special as the first. He pushed back from her lips and positioned himself between her thighs.

Then, gazing down into her passion-glazed eyes he said, "I will try not to hurt you, my love. But I feel my control slipping. Do you trust me, *meoon?*"

In a soft, trembling whisper she said, "Yes, my love. Oh, yes. I can't wait any more to be joined with you. "

So, taking hold of his shaft, he rubbed it between her folds and over her woman's nub until he heard her breaths coming in rapid pants and moans. She reached up, and as she ran her fingers through his hair, she cried out, "Now beloved, now!"

Pushing himself gently into her, he moved slowly until he felt her relax. Then, releasing his shaft, he entered her fully with one thrust. Mari cried out in ecstasy and he held her tight as she trembled in his arms.

"Hold onto me, Mari," moaned Thunder. "Hold tight as we fly to the stars."

She wrapped her legs around his thighs as he took hold of her bottom and pulled her to him to bury himself more fully within her. Then he began the age-old dance of love, and felt her orgasm over and over as he thrust hard for his own. Before long they both cried out in triumphant ecstasy as he spilled his seed deep within her. Then he collapsed, rolling them both to lie on their sides.

Still buried deep within her, he gazed at Mari's sated face. He felt that he had never seen a more beautiful woman in all his life, and began again to trail kisses across her neck and breasts.

In a trembling, husky pant. She stated,

"Oh, John, I love you so. I never knew life held such pleasure. All my friends long ago lied to me!"

John chuckled, as he nuzzled her breasts. "They didn't want you to know their secret. That they too felt pleasure during lovemaking, because white women think it's not proper to have such feelings. But we Cheyenne are taught that sexual pleasure is *Ma'heo'o's* greatest gift to lovers. So they would want to come together often thus making more children to keep the people strong."

"Well," she said as a radiant smile spread across her face, "I like your people's way better."

"Me too," he said. As he felt her stir beneath him, he again became hard.

As he slowly stroked within her, Mari stroked his shoulders and whispered in his ear, softly cooing, "Oh, that feels wonderful. Love me again and again my husband."

That was it. That was all it took for him to plunder her body with his hands and lips, and caress every inch of her again. He stroked within her as he teased her lips open with his tongue. He darted in and tasted her sweetness as he caressed and pumped within her.

They made love slowly this time, and rested within each other's arms as they lay before the fire. They would enjoy their feather bed tomorrow. Tonight was in sweet memory of the cabin by the sea— a fulfillment, a prophecy, and the fantasies that were born there between a Cheyenne Prince and a mermaid from the sea.

EPILOGUE

Sergeant O'Malley met with the council and went over all the ideas he had for settling Dream Valley. They were so thrilled that many of the men went with him and started right away, building a few cabins and laying out the grid plan for the town. Several families, after living in overcrowded dwellings, split up and settled there right away. William taught the young men that followed him the arts of building, engineering, and even some blacksmithing. Though trees and wood were scarce, they discovered quite by accident that certain shale rocks burned rather nicely, and William set about reinforcing the fireplaces in the dwellings to accommodate the higher temperatures.

Thunder and Mari became the proud parents of a beautiful baby girl they named Cyan. Mari said it meant "blue" like the sky.

They remained in Mist Valley, serving the people until the larger medical facility in Dream Valley was completed, and to Thunder's great joy, when Winter Blue went through his manhood rights, he was given the vision to also become a healer of the people like his father. Thunder swore he would teach his son well.

Billy Blue Hawk went to school and Black Crow felt he would someday accomplish his goal of becoming a newspaper man or even an author because he had such a gift at storytelling.

So all was peaceful and happy for a long time for the people of Dream Valley and Mist Valley, but just like life everywhere else, things were destined to undergo change and tragedy. In the white man's world to the south and east, a disease was spreading, and just as the Spirit Buffalo had told Thunder, it would eventually come to the people and he would be forced to fight the fight of his life... but that, my friends, is another tale set in a place called Dream Valley.

www.ingramcontent.com/pod-product-compliance
Lightning Source LLC
Chambersburg PA
CBHW060814120626
46557CB00001B/216